SUMMER SLASHER
HORROR ANTHOLOGY
VOL. 1

Edited by DCA and CBM

Springer Mountain Press
2021

Summer Slasher Horror Anthology
Edited by Clay Anderson

Copyright © 2021 by Springer Mountain Press

ISBN 978-1-7360898-4-2
Printed in USA by Springer Mountain Press
21 North Grove Street
Dahlonega, GA 30533
www.springermountainpress.com

Cover by Taylor Knecht
Interior by JW Manus

SUMMER SLASHER HORROR ANTHOLOGY

VOL. 1

EDITED BY DCA AND CBM

TABLE OF CONTENTS

Television

by Alyssa Hamilton

It had been a long day for you: commute in a downpour, unprepared summer students, mismatched shoes. The wetness got into your socks and stayed all day, never drying in the recesses of your loafer. You still felt the sinking squish as you walked up to the third floor of the apartment complex, the knot lodged in your right shoulder blade smarting of stress and rain. You knew which door to stop at without looking at the number, recognizing the particular smell of Pall Malls your brother liked. You opened it to reveal the smoke-murk of the living room.

"Dev?" you yelled into the bog you called home.

"What?" you heard his voice respond from the bathroom.

"You smoke indoors again? Remember what the guy from the landlord office said about that?"

"That sonofabitch can kiss my ass. He was a little shit in high school, and he thinks he can tell me how to live my life just because he's got this job."

You sighed and closed the door behind you. You stepped over the fallen stack of pizza boxes that littered the entryway to the kitchen, scouring the fridge for something quick to eat. There was nothing but a ring of mold left behind from a forgotten bunch of radishes, a half-empty carton of milk, assorted bottles of salad dressing, and ketchup. You called behind you, "Did you manage to go grocery shopping yet?"

"Too busy today," your brother answered, his voice closer than you expected.

You turned and found him leaning against the cabinets, robe open to reveal an old t-shirt and sweatpants. His jaw was rough with stubble. You asked, "Oh yeah? What'd you do?"

"Got caught up setting up the new TV." He cracked a smile, teeth dull.

Your brow furrowed. "New TV?"

"Yeah. I got it off Amazon. As a treat. My lawyer called the other day—looks like they're gonna settle my accident case for a nice chunk of change. They're gonna give us a number in a couple days."

"Oh really?" You cocked an eyebrow. You had heard that before.

"Yeah, really. It's gonna be soon, real soon. Just you wait and see. Hey, why you got on one black and one brown shoe?"

"It was dark when I got ready."

"You look ridiculous. You should take 'em off and watch TV. It's got internet and more channels than I know what to do with. I'm gonna go nap. Back's killing me." He shuffled towards the bedroom, crooked, socks charging with static as they rubbed against the carpet.

You shook your head, shut the refrigerator door. You dislodged your damp feet from their prisons, peeled your socks off, and left them in your shoes. You walked to the opposite side of the apartment and drew the curtains to let some light in, however stifled by rain it might have been. You watched the pooled water down below shiver as each drop disturbed its surface. You and your brother had been banned from using it after he had his outburst in May; your spine shrank as you remembered how loud your brother screamed at the other tenants and your relief when the mother of the boy he pushed didn't call the cops. By now, with August threatening heat lightning and sweat, you couldn't help but be thankful for this storm. The AC was shaky at best, and the ceiling fan made its best difference in this kind of weather.

You turned and sat on the futon, looking at your reflection in the black sheen of the dormant television. It was far bigger than you could have expected, nearly the entire length of the bookshelf. While it was a nice change from the bulky set your brother had brought from your childhood home—with this new LED sleekness like a Siren call of sloth—you were dreading the bill. You took a deep breath and turned it on.

Scrolling through dredges of reality TV, medical dramas, and local news channels, memories of eating frozen dinners on a tray came flooding back. You were no longer in that apartment—one moment, you were back in California, eating a burrito with your roommate as you pored over Chaucer for your Ph.D. program, reruns of *The Brady Bunch* providing background noise; another moment, you were watching *The Golden Girls* with your older sister as you waited for your first high school crush to pick you up for a movie. Sweeter moments, the ones when you were waiting for something better, like a kiss or the promise of a tenure-track job. Neither came.

Finally, a channel caught your eye, one you'd never seen before: ME. Maine? A pronoun? You clicked "select," curiosity piqued.

Your living room emerged from the sheen and static in all its glory: the ungraded paper piles, the garment rack full of Goodwill blazers, the chest filled with the blankets and pillows you used at night on the futon, all illuminated in HD. And you were there, too, sitting just as you were. You tilted your head. The you in the TV did not.

"What the hell?" you muttered.

TV you did not move your mouth.

A jolt of panic jabbed your chest. You had no security cameras, no webcams, nothing that could have been hacked to see the inside of the apartment. Was there something in the TV? Was it how your brother set it up?

TV you rose from your seat and glanced up at the ceiling fan whirling above in joyless merry-go-round motion. Arm raised, pulled the chain. The fan slowed and stopped. The face did not change; eyes remained locked. Belt peeled from hip-looped khaki. Braided leather became rope. Hands began to move in a way unknown to you before then, looping and pulling, knotting and slipping. A step on the coffee table. The section of rope opposite the noose wove above the fan's blades, came to another knot. Tug. Tug. Sturdy.

You tried to change the channel.

No button on the remote shed the images from the screen. TV you was expressionless, like the eyes of a deer watching before a fender smashed its legs. Head easily went through the noose, no stubbornness, not a single hair out of place. Legs kicked the coffee table out.

You shut your eyes. Your hands curled into fists. You shook your head as if motion was the cure for the sudden sway with no peace. But then there was a laugh track, a transatlantic accent making a joke about burning dinner. You looked back at the TV—a sitcom was playing. Husband and wife clad in suit and apron, shaking fingers at one another. And in your own hands, you found your belt.

"Can you believe the cook on this charter?" your brother asked, hand gesturing at the TV. Some soup spilled from his spoon, adding another stain to the carpet.

"Hmm?" you replied, your studying of your own bowl's pale green sea and chicken archipelago interrupted. You looked at Dev.

"Talking to the captain like that? If I ever talked to Coach like that, he'd've chewed my ass out. Like, what do you do if students talk to you like that?"

You shrugged. "Well, not much. Email one of the higher-ups. Then do whatever they tell me. Depends on the school, too. A couple of the ones I teach at in the falls are good about backing up part timers. Not all of them are, though."

Dev's eyebrows raised. "Really? I couldn't imagine . . ." He shook his head as he slurped a resistant noodle.

You smirked. "Like you never gave Mrs. Johnson a hard time in Chem?"

"Hey! That was different. I needed to graduate, and she was being a hard ass."

"Well, sometimes, I'm that hard ass."

"I mean, I guess that makes sense. You always were a teacher's pet. Can't say I'm all that surprised." His spoon clinked against his bowl.

You glanced at the glow above the bookcase, the clear waters somewhere off the coast of Greece. When one of the deckhands began to unravel a hose that looked too much like rope, you glanced away. "Hey, Dev? Can I ask you something?"

"Yeah, sure. Shoot."

"You ever . . . see something on TV . . . that's you?"

Dev leaned back against the futon and looked at you, cheeks inflated as he thought for a moment. Air sputtered out between his lips. "Like, what? Like I see something that reminds me of me?"

You shook your head. "No. Like you in the TV."

"You mean my reflection?" His head tilted.

"No . . . never mind. Maybe it was just my reflection and I was tired."

Dev shoved a loose fist against your shoulder. "Don't start losing it on me. One of us has to keep it together."

You chuckled and finished dinner in silence.

You sat in the lawyer's office next to the faux fig tree, its plastic leaves reflecting light in a waxen glare. The receptionist's nails clicked against the keyboard as she took a message. The local news station detailed the incoming heat wave. It was the typical, taupe drone of this waiting room. You pulled papers out of your briefcase, unsheathing your red pen from its compartment.

". . . and expect severe thunderstorms early next week," the muted suit predicted from the TV mounted in the corner.

You shook your head as you began reading, dreading the upcoming plague of worms smearing across the sidewalks at campus. The pop of flesh bursting beneath your shoe always stiffened your spine.

Just as you clicked your pen to grade the first essay, the receptionist's nails no longer ticked. The weatherman no longer prophesized. The AC no longer whirred, yet your skin bumped and itched as if January was breathing down your neck. You looked up. And it was the same as it had been a couple days ago.

The television was not reflecting the waiting room. There was no rack of magazines, no basket bearing fig tree or succulents, no iron-armed chairs seen in thousands of incarnations across the purgatory states of law or medicine. You were looking at your living room again, at the futon and table, and you—you sitting there, the features of your face obscured. But you could tell, despite the depth of the eye sockets, that you were meeting your own gaze.

And you rose and stood on the coffee table again. The rope was there already, hanging from the ceiling fan out of frame. The loop grazed your cheek—you turned to look at it. The fabric beneath you became rough like the sting of rope-fray, like wheat or thistle or thorn. Your head bowed and slipped through as if to teach a child, *yes, this is where the circle goes! This is where the circle will always be meant to go.*

"Ready to go?" Dev's voice suddenly interrupted.

You shook your head, finding Dev standing by the receptionist's desk. "Oh . . . oh? Already?"

Dev didn't look at you when he answered. "Yeah. Let's go."

You reached down for your briefcase, realizing that you were already standing.

⸺⸺⸺

You stared into the plastic bowl of rice and cheese, examining the melting strings, how it didn't quite lose the artificial sheen it had out of the package. The sports documentary droned on in the background, the commentator's voice marveling at the Steelers in the 1970s.

"You ever wish you could have been there?" Dev asked.

You looked up at him, turning your gaze to his face. He was still engrossed in the grainy footage glowing from the screen, the image doubled too perfectly in the slick of his eye. "Huh? Sorry, I was thinking of something else."

He didn't look away to answer you. "You ever watch or read about something that happened and wish you could've been there? Like, who was that dude you did that project on in grad school?"

"My dissertation? William Dunbar?"

"Yeah. Do you ever wish you were there when he was writing?" His face tinted green as the footage played a game highlight, returning some color to his cheeks.

You continued to look at his profile as you answered him, "Well, I guess so."

"Written with him?" he asked.

You leaned back against the futon. "I don't know about that."

"I'd kill to be on the 1972 Steelers. I'd've been drafted with Franco Harris." His lips spread into a wide grin, his face glowing then with fantasy as he must have been picturing himself tackling someone to protect Harris. "The two of us would've done it together. Could you see me doing that?" The smile didn't completely fade from his mouth when he stopped talking.

"I mean, before that lady hit you—"

Dev's eyes hardened, jaw tensed. The light dimmed on his face. "No. We're not talking about that. We're talking about me and Harris winning Super Bowls together. Making all that money. Buying houses and shit. Giving interviews, having people listen to what we gotta say. Doing what we were born to do. Could you imagine? Doing what you were born to do?"

You studied Dev. His gaze did not meet yours, too absorbed in the documentary to notice you staring at him. You asked, "Are you okay? You seem . . . off tonight."

He shook his head. "I'm fine, I'm fine. Just thinking is all."

"Look, I know the number the insurance company gave wasn't great, but didn't the lawyer give you some hope? Like there's just some more documents you can give him to help prove the case—"

"No." His face was smoothed to fresh concrete.

"Look, there's still more we can do. I get paid again at the end of the month, and I picked up another class for the fall, so don't worry. I can cover the copay, we can go see that specialist and see what they say. I'll help you go through your records and organize them. It'll be okay."

His face remained blank. "You're right. It'll be okay. It'll all be okay."

"Good. Don't worry. We'll be okay."

You were heating up lunch in the faculty lounge's kitchenette when the Dean of Arts and Sciences came in and sat on one of the many worn chairs, salad in hand. She noticed you tucked in the corner and nodded, lips pursed in a half-cordial, half-unenthused smile. You returned the gesture. She began to flip through the stations on the mounted television, landing on one of the old movie channels. She quickly whipped her head from side to side, a crack erupting from between her vertebrae. You cringed and shifted your focus to the soup turning in the microwave like a lethargic ballerina bathed in dull light.

"It's funny. I've never actually seen the end of *Casablanca*," she said.

"Really?" you asked.

"I've seen it in bits and pieces, but never sat down and watched it from start to finish. Harold is teaching a new course on film in the 1940s and is using it. Have you seen it?"

"No. I've been watching a lot of science fiction lately."

"Always good."

You continued to examine the ballerina pregnant with vegetable broth and noodles. Cold sweat began to emerge from the nape of your neck, lower intestine feeling like a fork twirling pasta around its prongs. You rose your head to look at her again. "So, has the President made the decision about the new faculty positions?"

She glanced at you, smiling. "It's funny you mention that. She approved the new position in the English department. The posting goes live tomorrow among current employees. You should apply. Your name came up in a meeting." She paused. "Isn't this strange?"

"What do you mean?" you asked.

She wasn't looking at you—she was looking at the television. "Isn't *It's a Wonderful Life* a Christmas movie?"

"It is."

"Then why is it on now?"

You followed her gaze to the screen. To you, there was no snow. There were no prayers being spoken.

There was no cosmos assigning miracles between flaring stars. There was only the figure standing on the coffee table in your apartment, bowls littered about its feet in technicolor clutter. The rope hung from the fan. A blacked-out face went through the rope like thread through a needle, like a finger through a ring, like an act of love. Your neck felt the compression as the rope nuzzled against your throat, its fibers smoothed and uniform, organized like spirals of petals to form chrysanthemum. The table was kicked out. Bowls bounced against the carpet. A snap. A swing. A soft sway. A single streamer leftover from a party.

It had been a better day for you: a commute without traffic, a chatty class, shoes that fit better than they ever had before. One of your neighbors nodded at you in the parking lot, the mother of that boy your brother pushed. She smiled at you. You returned it, warmth crinkling your eyes, jaw feeling stretched and soothed. Birds darted between shrubs in front of the door to your building—cardinals diving and finches avoiding their paths. Sun was no blistering nuisance. A slight breeze tamed it.

You couldn't smell the Pall Malls as you ascended the stairs to your floor. Maybe your brother was finally quitting like he said he would. Maybe he'd feel better once you told him what the Dean said. You opened the door. All things fled from your mind when your eyes met his—your own mirrored in the dull-slick stillness.

A rope swayed from the ceiling fan.

A Stake Through the Heart

by Ann Hite

The world was filled with blood: roiling, boiling, unending sticky red-ness. Or so thought Miss Arlene Bradshaw, who spent most Satur-day nights watching scary movies. This contributed to her overactive imagination and her firm belief that something evil was in Holly Io-wa's house next door. Arlene, Holly's dearest, oldest friend, was not allowed inside to see for herself. But that sure didn't keep her from trying. Arlene worked at gaining entrance into her friend's house for a whole week, but Holly, wrapped in one of her silky robes, shooed her away.

Oh, Holly was real polite. "Now, Arlene, honey, I'm just too busy to have you over now. You'll have to come back some other time."

Arlene was sure some conjure spell had ahold of Holly—she looked like warmed-over death, all gray around the eyes—but Arlene was a good Christian neighbor, by gosh. She taught Sunday school at Black Mountain Baptist Church going on thirteen years. Her welcome at Holly's was worn out. Nobody had to hit her in the head with a brick. That was just fine. Let some old witches get Holly. Arlene washed her hands of the whole mess. Instead, Arlene drove down the mountain that Friday night in late June to see a show. Mostly, Holly always went with her and they saw the newest movie in Asheville. Holly loved her some Elvis. The way he shook his hips made both Holly and Arlene giggle like teenagers. Neither of them was ever married, and now they were hugging forty and getting too dern old for men to want to marry them. Arlene wasn't a bit bothered. Men just made her feel stupid, and she much preferred church and scary movies to such, but Holly wanted her a man. She talked about it all the time. She even started taking a correspondence vocabulary course to get smarter, as if smarts captured a man. Too bad for Holly because she was the size of Mrs. Connor's milk cow. No man wanted a cow for a wife. So, they were stuck on the mountain together except Holly quit coming out of her house. Arlene worried it might be because she asked Holly what the fancy vocabulary word for cow was.

Arlene drove her car by Holly's house real slow on the way to the picture show. The curtains were pulled tight. That just wasn't like Holly to keep them shut on such a fine evening. She stopped the car for one more try to gain entry.

The curtain moved when Arlene got out of the car. She marched up the steps and beat on the door like there was a fire. A giggle came from the other side. Did Holly think Arlene couldn't hear? She beat on the door again for good measure. Silence.

The door cracked open. Holly stood in her robe. "Arlene honey, what do you want today?"

Wearing a robe in the evening was just downright tacky. "I come to take you to a movie. Get out of that robe and come on."

Holly's face was pale. The lack of natural daylight was starting to take its toll on her tan. She made a huffing sound. "I done told you,

Arlene Bradshaw, I'm busy. Now don't make me be rude." She closed the door.

Arlene stomped down the stairs. Never in her life had anyone been so mean. What was that woman's problem? She got into her car and drove down the mountain to see the new Elvis movie alone.

The theater in Asheville looked like a grand affair with fancy chandelier lights and high ceilings, so it was just a pleasure to visit. And there was the best of news on the marquee: *When Vampires Meet Werewolves*. Arlene bought a big bag of popcorn. That would show stupid old Holly not to come with her to the movies. Not thirty minutes into the movie, Arlene saw Holly's problem plain as day. My Lord, a vampire had gotten her. Nothing could be more obvious. Holly didn't come out in the daylight. She looked like a walking dead person. Arlene paid closer attention to the movie. Vampires could turn themselves into bats and fly through windows. That's exactly how he got Holly. She always left her windows open at night. Arlene had told her over and over and over that it was 1967 and folks just couldn't go around with all the doors unlocked and the windows open, but, no, Holly hadn't listened to a word. She had laughed at Arlene. Well, that was her just reward. Now, she was a dern vampire, and Arlene would have to expose her to sunlight, drive a wooden stake through her heart, or shoot her with a silver bullet. No, wait, that was for killing a werewolf.

On the drive home, a full moon hung in the sky. When Arlene passed Holly's house, she noticed a floodlight on in the backyard. A shadow moved around. She killed the headlights on her car and found the courage deep in her chest to creep through the underbrush until she saw a man wearing a cape digging a hole. Of course, it was a bunch of shadows so she could have been wrong, but, one thing was for sure, the sound of the scraping of a shovel in the dirt was there. The man was digging a grave. Maybe the pastor could help. He was the closest thing Black Mountain had to a sheriff, but, just at that moment, big old Holly stepped out on her back porch right into the floodlight like she was on a stage. She was wearing a red dress and her face was made up like some woman of the night. Of course, Arlene would never say a thing like that to her best friend.

"Are you finished with that digging?" Holly's voice sounded off key like she was trying to sing instead of talk.

"It should be ready for planting in the next couple of days. Then all you have to do is wait and pick them."

Oh my, the blood beat in Arlene's head. Did the man say victim? Or pick them? A bat swept through the sky. Arlene ran for her life to the car. The vampires were looking for a victim. They would choose her. She was the logical person. No real family. No one to notice she had disappeared for a few days. Arlene had to put an end to the whole mess.

In her kitchen, she made a good old-fashion garlic necklace. Granny always made them to ward off disease, but now Arlene understood that Granny knew about vampires that live forever. The same vampire who got Holly could have been around when Granny was young. Arlene hung the garlic around her neck and went to bed, but sleep came hard. She was sure someone was walking around downstairs. Yes. This was a time for Arlene to take things in her own hands. No one believed in vampires anymore.

The next morning Arlene went to see old Betty, the conjuring woman. If she was going to rid Black Mountain of vampires, she had to make sure to do it right. Betty sat on her front porch swing, fanning herself with a funeral home fan.

"Good morning, Miss Arlene. What you doing out so early on a Saturday?"

"I wanted to ask you some questions."

"Well, depends on what kind. Some questions cost money."

"I know. I got some questions about vampires. You're the conjuring woman. You have to know some of these answers."

Betty stopped fanning herself. "What did you say?"

"Vampires. I got questions about vampires."

"Lord, that's going to cost fifty cents apiece. You're asking about real secrets."

"I'll pay." Arlene opened her purse.

"Ok. Shoot."

"Have you ever known a vampire to be around the mountain?"

Betty relaxed into the swing. "Never. And understand, I would know if one of those evil things was here."

"So you say. I just wonder." Arlene took two quarters out of her change purse and placed them on Betty's palm. "I think you might be losing your skill."

Betty gave her a hard look. "Got any more?"

"How do you know if a person is a vampire?"

Betty sucked in a deep breath. "I ain't going to charge you for that question cause I done said no vampires are on this mountain."

"Ok then. How about the best way to get rid of a vampire?"

"Daylight will turn them to dust. But the best way is to drive a stake into their heart. A stake made from an apple tree. That's the best." She held out her hand. "That's going to be a dollar because you got two answers."

Arlene plucked a dollar from her wallet. "Thank you, Betty. That was very helpful."

"You be careful with that information, girl."

Arlene purely hated to cut the low limb on her apple tree, but something had to be done. The job took her a good hour. Then she took the limb to Tyler Morgan. He was best with wood. "I want you to make me a sturdy stake."

He gave her a funny look over the top of his glasses. "Why?"

"So I can drive it into a vampire's chest. Why else?" She laughed.

He laughed, slapping his knee. "You watch too many of those scary movies, Arlene. I'll have it ready this afternoon."

"Good."

"When I get through with this stake, it'll hold the biggest tomatoes on Black Mountain."

"Just make the point good and sharp." She gave a half smile. "So I can drive it into the ground without a problem."

Arlene took her hammer along with the stake and crossed through the patch of woods that separated her yard from Holly's. The house was shut up tight, but that didn't matter a bit because Arlene had Holly's spare key.

The house was stuffy and dark. Clothes were thrown here and there. Burnt candles sat all over the living room and kitchen. Arlene couldn't believe her eyes. Holly kept a perfect house. This was proof she was not herself. Arlene started down to the cellar but heard a muffled sound from upstairs. She tiptoed, holding her tools of destruction. Moans that sounded like a cat in heat came from Holly's bedroom. Arlene stood in front of the door. This was her friend probably dying.

She had to go in there and save her. The door flew open with more force than she thought she had.

Both Holly and ugly Fred Harper—he lived two farms over and was known all over the mountain for how ugly he was—were tangled up in the bed sheets. What in the world was going on? The sight of a naked, overweight woman and a pure ugly man struck her dumb.

Holly got her bearings, and her face turned purple with rage. "Arlene Bradshaw. This is the end of our friendship. I can't believe you just came in my house uninvited."

"What in the world you got a hammer and a stake for, Miss Arlene?" Fred was a right proper man even when he didn't have a stitch of clothes on.

"I was going to put in some tomatoes, but I can't drive this stake in the ground. I knew Holly was good at putting in gardens. I thought she might help me. But she's been unreasonable all week, so I just let myself in." Arlene gave Holly a grin. "I guess that vocabulary class paid off after all."

Holly pointed her big old finger at the door. "Get on home, Arlene. Now." She knew Arlene better than anyone, and that would never change.

Best Friends Forever

by Mark Braught

Leaves change color, nights grow longer, the air more relaxed, and Halloween is close. It's the welcome reward for surviving the unbearable heat and stifling humidity of summer in northern Georgia. Sacred southern traditions of football and festivals usher in the season.

I hail from a predominantly rural county with several covered bridges. This was a good excuse as any to create one of those festivals. These century-old wooden structures, off the beaten paths of progress and paved, laned roads, are evidence that connect us to a much slower time as well as both sides of the creeks they span. The locals gather, and big-city folk will wander out for a few days to pick up some homemade knick-knacks, local cuisine, and collectibles of yesteryear.

One bridge in particular captures the young imaginations of the area and looms large in every child's curiosity and darkest dreams: the Concord Bridge over Nickajack Creek. Initially built in 1848, burned down by Sherman's troops on their march to Savannah in 1864, and rebuilt on the very same footings in 1872.

Every year, Teri K. Holbrook, my childhood friend, and I meet

Halloween on this bridge at midnight. We catch up, eat candy, and, most importantly, challenge the local legend that has been passed on from generation to generation to see who will lose their courage and retreat. This is our tradition. It is my job to bring the candy and her duty to supply the courage. Inevitably, no matter how much she provides, there is never enough of that courage to help me outlast her.

The legend goes that at some time, long ago, there was an asylum, a place for unwanted children, now long gone, somewhere in the woods around Nickajack Creek. The tale reports that these children were left to themselves with little or no care, and many died of starvation and neglect. The institution is closed and long abandoned, but it is widely believed the spirits of those unfortunate lost souls and every other youth that passed away in these woods reside under the bridge, still looking for sweet treats to eat. Never forget your candy if you venture out there at night. You might just disappear as well!

Each year, and there have been many now, I come back to the stomping grounds of my youth to visit family, see how the town has not really changed all that much, but primarily to see Teri. How is she? Has she changed any? I remember her as that curious, courageous force of nature that I looked up to and felt that if I were around her enough, I might become brave too. Maybe she needed to lead someone as much as I needed to be that someone to follow. Together, we were a duo, facing challenges and adventures she would create. Climbing trees, running farther, jumping higher, and exploring unknown nooks and crannies of our little town. We marveled at the curiosities we discovered. These memories of our friendship are why she remains my dearest friend. Teri is the indispensable reason I return every year.

Evening is gone, and the dead of night is here. I have a growing anxiety preparing for our annual reunion. There's not much to do, but

I have to make sure I have enough of our favorite Moon Pies for both of us. A large, full, bright moon and clear night sky light the way as I begin hiking to the Concord Bridge. It's down a dirt and gravel road, just outside of town, edged by large, looming white oaks, pecan trees, and a growing fog tonight. Only slight whispering breezes and pesky gnats interrupt my thoughts and the knot in my stomach. How will she surprise me this year? She takes way too much pleasure scaring the be-gezzes out of me. I know it's coming. Don't know when. I know it will be quick. Of course it will be painless, but it has become our weird sort of "hello" and a reminder to us both that I am still the Robin to her Batman. Some things can't change.

Arriving at the bridge, my footsteps echo on the wooden floor-boards. I move a few steps forward into the structure. Cautiously stop-ping to look around, I bark into the dark, "HELLO! . . . Teri?"

Teri is nowhere to be seen. Where is she hiding? Venturing for-ward even more, I inspect every inch of the walls, left and right and right to left, until I arrive at the center of the bridge. I'm going to stand my ground here and wait. Where is she hiding? All I can hear are muffled sounds of the current of the creek below my feet. Inside my head, I reassure myself, "I've got this covered. Strategically I can see her coming from any direction in time to avoid being scared out of my wits. This is my year!"

Silence, me, and the dark are waiting, occasionally asking the ob-vious question out loud. "Teri?"

Eventually, too much time has passed, and I'm starting to believe she isn't coming this year. "I hope she's OK." I consider, but, between us, I am coming to the conclusion my friend isn't going to come. She has other things to do, or people to see, or just *stuff* more important than us.

Feeling rejected and more than a little hurt, I drop my head, slide my hands into my pockets, and turn to leave. Lifting my eyes to get a bearing on the road, I'm practically lifted out of my shoes in fear!

"DAMN IT, TERI!"

There she is. Standing there quietly behind me, patiently waiting for that inevitable moment I would turn around and jump out of my skin.

Gathering my wits and composure, I reluctantly offer up a "well done" acknowledgment.

Teri doesn't disappoint. She is still the same. Her eyes are twinkling with mischief, and, without a word, that familiar, slightly sly grin is proclaiming her victory. Yep, she hasn't changed a bit. It's so good to see her again. Quickly, I produce Moon Pies from my pocket for both of us, and together we unwrap and nibble our treats. We just stand silent, looking at each other intensely while chewing away. Each tick is precious and treasured. Every moment so profound I refuse to blink, fearing some detail will be missed.

Finally, I can't contain it any longer.

"It's so good to see you," I whisper, confident it will begin a conversation. This is not going to be. She lowers the confection from her lips and grins, beaming from ear to ear, bobbing her head in agreement. These minutes have the illusion of eternity.

Reluctantly, time catches up to us and the night air regains its chill. Our moment is slipping away, and Teri is gently beginning to transform. Initially gradually disappearing, then slowly dissolving and becoming more and more transparent, thinning herself, smiling all the while. With one last wave good-bye, she completely evaporates and vanishes, becoming part of the night fog, and is gone. Alone on the bridge, there's nothing to do but retreat back to town, but not in fear.

Wandering back home, my thoughts are about our friendship and the unfortunate drowning incident that took Teri's life so many years ago in the Nickajack Creek under the Concord Bridge.

I don't know why Teri shows up every year. I'm not exactly sure why I do. The doubters in the group will believe it's all about a far too vivid imagination or that she can't resist the temptation of the free sweet treat. Fondly, I prefer to think it is Teri's way of reassuring me she is doing well on the other side and is my best friend forever.

SINISTER FACES IN THE DARK

by Annie James

Jonah was in his room at Alpha Frat House, nearly finished typing his thirty-page essay, when the lights went out, instantly plunging the room into thick darkness and heavy silence. "Damn!" He growled as he quickly saved his work and then grabbed a flashlight from his top desk drawer to search for the fuse box. The light and noise woke his girlfriend Janelle, who had fallen asleep in his bed after watching a movie. Jonah hadn't been tired, so he had gotten up to finish his paper.

"What's going on?" Janelle asked sleepily.

"Nothing, the power went out. Go back to sleep, I'm just going to find the fuse box." Janelle nodded and lowered her head to the pillow again.

The instant Jonah stepped out of his room, he ran into a body—a living one, thankfully. "Gaah!" Jonah yelled and heard a stranger scream too. Jonah aimed the flashlight at the face of the other person, relaxing when he saw it was only his frat brother Dan.

"Dude, you scared me," Jonah said. "Where is the fuse box?"

"Man, do I look like an electrician? I was coming to ask you."

"Great." Jonah sighed in disgust. "C'mon, help me find it. Let's check the kitchen."

In the kitchen they found another frat brother, Kevin, already examining the breaker box with a flashlight.

"Look at this crap!" Kevin shouted. "I mean, what the . . . it's melted."

"What do you mean, melted?" Jonah asked.

Kevin raised his eyebrows and gestured toward the switches, jiggling one to show them that it wouldn't move. "The plastic switches are melted." He shined his flashlight on the misshapen lumps of plastic, which were fused into the off position.

"I didn't know electricity could do that," Dan said, scratching his goatee in confusion. "Dude, forget this. Let's go to that party where the other guys are and report this in the morning."

That sounded good to Kevin and Jonah, so the trio headed for the front door only to find it wouldn't open. Jonah twisted the handle back and forth, confirming it was not locked. "What the heck is this?" Kevin asked, shining his flashlight up toward the top of the door. The light illuminated three long nails that had been pounded into the top of the door frame and twisted down to keep the front door from being opened.

"Woah, what is going on?!" Dan asked, his high-pitched tone indicating that he was starting to freak out.

"We need a hammer to pull these out," Jonah said. "Kevin, you have some tools, do you have a hammer?"

"Yeah, I'll be right back," Kevin said, and he headed upstairs.

Jonah shined his flashlight on the nails that had been pounded into the door frame. "Let's hope. I have a bad feeling, though. Someone in here nailed this door shut. We need to find out what is going on."

"Maybe the other guys are playing a prank?" Dan asked, sounding hopeful. Jonah just shook his head.

"I don't think this is a prank. Besides, the other guys are at the party. It's only you, me, and Kevin here."

On a typical night, the frat house would be full of boisterous sounds, stereos blaring, tv's playing, chatter, laughter. Tonight, the silence was ominous, and when there was a loud, abrupt crash and thud from upstairs, they heard it clearly.

"What was that?" Dan whispered.

"I don't know," Jonah whispered back.

"Are you ok, Kev?!" Dan suddenly shouted in the silence.

Jonah clapped his hand over Dan's mouth. "Shut up, idiot! Now whoever is in here knows where we are! C'mon." Jonah pulled Dan towards the kitchen. "We need to get away from the front door."

Jonah pulled out his phone to call 911, but it said there was no service. "Oh no, why isn't it working? Maybe they are using a cell phone jammer."

"Let's go find Kevin and get out of here!" Dan whispered frantically.

Jonah nodded, and they moved toward the stairs. He clicked off the flashlight. Dan gasped, but Jonah swatted him. "I don't want the intruder to see the light," Jonah whispered. "Step carefully."

There was light coming in the windows, allowing them to see. It was still dim inside, though, so the staircase was drowned in shadow.

The upstairs was much darker. Jonah turned the flashlight back on, this time keeping it mostly covered by his hand so that it would remain dim while still allowing them to see. Jonah spotted a dark puddle on the floor outside of Kevin's door. He took a chance and shined his light on it, and he and Dan recoiled in horror when they saw it was blood. A trail of blood led from the door to the back staircase, which led down to the garage door on one side and the cellar door on the other.

"I think Kevin is dead, man," Dan whispered.

"Sshh. He might still be alive, I hope," Jonah replied. "C'mon."

Jonah started down the stairs.

"I'm not going down there," Dan hissed, and he turned back and rushed into Kevin's room. It sounded like he locked the door and put a chair under the handle.

"Chicken shit," Jonah said under his breath. *I should have grabbed a weapon*, Jonah thought. *At least I have an idea where the intruder is.* He continued to follow the blood trail down the stairs. *I can find a weapon in the garage.*

At the bottom of the stairs, the blood trail led to the cellar door. *Kevin must be down there, and the intruder is probably down there with him.* Jonah quietly opened the door leading to the garage and stepped through, pulling it shut behind him.

He looked around for a suitable weapon and saw a bat propped up in a corner, so he grabbed that and stepped back into the house. He had just put his hand on the basement doorknob when he heard Janelle scream from upstairs.

Without a second thought, he turned and rushed back to his room. He kicked the door in, and Janelle backed against the wall, eyes wide with fear. Jonah shined the flashlight on his face so she would recognize him, and then she rushed into his arms, sobbing.

"Jonah! There's someone in the house . . . a guy . . . he ran away when he heard you coming up the stairs. He has a knife, he cut my arm."

"It's ok, you're safe now. Which way did he go?"

"I don't know, down the back stairs maybe?"

"Come with me, I'll take care of this."

He took Janelle's hand, and they headed quietly toward the back staircase. They crept down the stairs, which thankfully didn't creak.

Jonah carefully opened the door to the basement and listened. He didn't hear anything. He turned to Janelle and put his finger to his lips. She was still quietly crying, and she tried to muffle the sound with her hand.

Jonah dimmed the flashlight beam with his hand and led Janelle down the narrow wooden steps. At the bottom, he shined his flashlight beam around carefully. The light caught the unconscious form of Kevin, duct taped to an old chair.

Jonah went over to him and tried to shake him awake, but Kevin's head just lolled onto his chest and he didn't respond. Jonah moved the flashlight over him, looking for injuries, and he noticed a small puncture wound in Kevin's neck.

"I think he was injected with something," Jonah whispered to Janelle. "We have to get help. There is another exit—storm cellar doors—I've seen them from the outside." Jonah looked around. "Over there, c'mon." Jonah hurried over the unused part of the basement and up a short flight of four steps. He pushed up on the double doors, but they moved only a few inches. He could see that the handles were chained together from the outside.

"We are going to have to find another way out, Janelle."

"Yeah, not going to happen," Janelle said, laughter in her tone.

A male voice started laughing, and a boulder of dread formed in Jonah's stomach.

Jonah turned around to see her grinning, her arm around a guy who looked just like Jonah, except he wore a mocking smile.

"Jesse?" Jonah said, shocked.

Jesse cocked his head to the side. "Did you miss me, brother?" Jesse drew out the syllables in a mocking tone.

Jesse turned to Janelle. "I'm sorry for cutting you babe, but you know we had to sell this." They kiss. Then, Janelle turned to Jonah and said, "No hard feelings. I really do like you, but I met Jesse first."

"How?" Jonah asked, shocked.

"I was a nurse at the mental hospital where he was a patient. I enrolled here as a pre-med student to get close to you and then helped my sweetheart escape."

"Why are you doing this?"

"I'm going to become you, brother, and now it's your turn to find out what it is like to be locked in a mental ward."

"You deserve it," Janelle chimes in. "Keeping your darling brother locked up!"

"They are going to know I'm not you! Mom and Dad will . . ."

"Your parents are dead; I took care of them already." Janelle smirked.

Jonah despaired hearing this. *The tattoo,* Jonah thought. He had just gotten it a couple of days ago, a sword on the back of his shoulder.

As if she was reading his mind, Janelle said, "He even got a tattoo yesterday, just like the one you have. Oh yeah, I told him about that, too." Janelle grinned evilly. "One last thing to do," Janelle said as she pulled out her phone.

Dialing 911, she burst into frantic tears, pretending to hyperventilate. "Oh god, please send the police! An intruder broke into the frat house at NYU. I'm hiding from him, so I can't stay on the phone, please send help." Janelle hung up the phone and her tears immediately stopped. Then, Janelle held a knife to Kevin's throat, and said she would kill him if Jonah didn't cooperate.

He had no choice but to let Jesse duct tape him to a chair. When the police arrived, Janelle told them that Jonah was the escaped mental patient. Jonah tried to tell him who he was, but there was no one to vouch for him. They strapped him to a gurney in the ambulance and gave him an injection to make him sleepy. The last thing Jonah saw was the ambulance doors closing.

Quell the Voices

by Ann Hite

A Puzzle 1995

When Bess Pritchard left her body that windy March afternoon, it was as if her heart tore open, and she took the form of black, oily smoke hugging the ceiling of the house. Was this real? Her spirit moved through the maze of outdated newspapers, broken-down pasteboard boxes, and empty two-liter diet soda cartons—saved with the crazy notion she might win some contest advertised on them.

Bess took the form of a deep black crow, so black the wings appeared navy blue in the sunlight. A young woman, standing on the sidewalk, witnessed the transformation of oily smoke to wings spread. Bess flew to the top of a water oak, where she gathered in the changes. Her life broken into several pieces resembled a jigsaw puzzle with key gaps, untold stories. The missing parts danced out of reach like a deep ache in her bones.

The pretty young woman on the sidewalk below shielded her eyes to the sun, staring at her, the crow. How had this trendy girl, perfect hair, clothes that were made just for her, come to the backward community of Black Mountain?

Two men wheeled a gurney with her body on it out the front door. Both the men, broad shoulders, big hands the right size to crush the skull of a child, wore expressions of disgust.

Hopeless Choices 1974

Bess's daughter was removed from her home four days after her second birthday, not that Bess even celebrated the event. The little girl cried all the time, causing pressure to build in Bess's skull. The money was gone, and she was alone, except for the child. No husband. He never existed. The daughter's birthday came and went with only a ripple of dread, regret, as Bess watched the sunset from her dingy boarding room. She tried to recall the birth in detail, but only felt lonely blackness where memories should have resided.

The daughter watched Bess from the back window of the car marked with the state seal, searching Bess's face with liquid black eyes, no tears, only a look of expectation. The girl was leaving the single room above old Widow Dobson's store. It was the widow who called Children Services when the child cried too much. Bess hit the child, squeezed her little head with her hand until she finally turned quiet, and her eyes grew larger, shuttered. A blue bruise appeared on each side of her head. This incident, coupled with leaving the girl alone to earn money, brought Bess into the situation. The state woman had pushed papers into Bess's face, forcing her way past, gathering the girl in her arms, leaving Bess to read the verdict.

Instead of the expected relief, Bess cried as the car pulled away, and she lost her reason for living, for trying to live, her one and only hope.

What possessed her to place so much hope in her ability to be a mother? That night in the dirty bed, her last night there, Mama came and stood beside Bess, judging the deeds that placed Bess there. For a long time, Bess wandered the streets of Asheville, hoping to see the car that took the little girl away. At night, as she sat under a tree in someone's yard, her daughter's tiny face appeared in Bess's dreams. She longed for the warm body snuggled beside her. Within months the girl's face blurred in her mind and life blended into weeks, months, one moment of choice. Whisky numbed her mind, her heart. Scales formed over her eyes and needles left their marks on her arms and legs.

Recognition 1995

The men from the funeral home, sweat stains marking their freshly pressed shirts, squatted in unison to hoist the gurney with Bess's body into the back of the hearse.

"Look at the back tires on that thing." Red Connor, the larger of the two men, his red hair thinner than she remembered, but still looking youthful, grinned at the other man. His family owned the one and only funeral home on the mountain. Once upon a time, Bess knew every inch of Red's body, each mole and freckle. Not out of love, no, out of need, a need to feed a hunger for contact, of forgetting. Carlton always lacked when it came to touching, keeping his distance. Even at that moment, the thought brought guilt flooding into her body. Carlton had been so good to her. Hadn't he?

But the young woman drew Bess out of those thoughts. Her eyes reminded her of someone.

Savior 1976

Carlton Weehunt found Bess in a gutter in the worst part of Asheville. He wore the look of a backwards man, inside of his head most of the time. He was the type Bess recognized as predictable to the point of danger. His hands, long slender fingers, like a girl's, drew her attention. His eyes were so brown they looked black. His thick beard was neat, but his hair went a little wild. Something deep inside stirred, grew, when she concentrated too hard on his stare.

"Girl, what you sitting in the filth for?" His voice soft, matter of fact.

"I don't give a damn anymore. I've ridden this horse so long it owns me, and now I'd be better off dead."

He stood looking down at her, an inner fight passing over his face. His pocketknife was produced and he ran his finger over the case, flipping out the blade, pointing it at her. "It seems to me you got two choices."

Bess's heart hammered with familiarity, a welcome release.

"You can take this knife here and slit your own throat. It ain't so bad to die that way. Or you can get up and follow me home. No more drugs. No more liquor. Home to Black Mountain. Do you remember Black Mountain? Your mama, Sally, left you her house. I'll help you to get clean."

The knife blade had brown splotches here and there. Bess laughed. She could almost feel the weight in her hand. She had turned into a decaying, crumbling skeleton. This man thought he could help such a creature as if he was some kind of god, as if she could go home.

"Go away. God wouldn't have me. Why would you? I can't go to that mountain. I'm dirty."

"Who brought God into this? It seems I'm your only option." His eyes reflected anything but a holy presence. A familiar glint persuaded her to see things his way, as if a similar scene in the past dictated this only response.

In her saner moments, Bess would go on to wonder if she had remained in that gutter and rode her addiction to the end, would the results have been better, a shorter life, less time to experience the pain and insanity?

Natural Causes 1995

The big-bellied sheriff paced back and forth in front of Bess's house. Why was he in her yard?

"There ain't much to say about Bess. Her daddy was one of the best men this mountain ever knew. Funny how those kinds of things work. Bess was on the mountain most of her life, but left for a bit when her mama died. Lots of us do, but no one ever knew where she went or what she did. Folks around here look after one another, and they did their duty by Bess. All her family were dead or gone by that time. She just wasn't the same girl that left here. You know what I mean? It's like she left a piece of her mind out there off the mountain."

The young woman took off her slick black coat and glanced at the crow, Bess, sitting in the tree. "Didn't anyone around here attempt to get her some help? Don't you wonder why she died?"

"It looks like natural causes to me. You saw her weight. I don't mean to be rude, ma'am, but what's all this to you?" The sheriff pulled a notebook from his pocket and scribbled something on the page with a short, chewed-on pencil.

"Bess Pritchard was my mother."

Had Bess heard this right? She studied the woman's face, the dark eyes, faded to a hazel color, no longer liquid. Could her child have transformed into this beautiful creature?

The sheriff stopped writing and looked at the woman. "That can't be. Bess never married, never had a boyfriend. The mountain would have known."

Red stepped away from the hearse. "I'm ready to roll."

Bess never thought he'd speak up, own his involvement.

The woman laughed. "I don't think I have to tell you that babies can be brought into the world without a marriage."

"Where were you born?"

"I was hoping Ms. Pritchard could answer that question for me. After the state took me in Asheville, Bess dropped off the face of the earth. It took my adoption a long time to go through without a birth certificate."

"Bess stayed gone for four years. Her daddy died early in her life. Her mama married again but Bess never got close to him. He disappeared after Bess did."

"Why did her father die so young?"

"Connor died when a tractor flipped over on him. Bess watched. Never was the same."

Guilty as Charged 1976

The smell of bacon worked its way into the bedroom, causing Bess to gag. Carlton had brought her back to the mountain, the farmhouse where she grew up. Everywhere she looked, she saw her mother and father. She gagged again. Where was the sweet numbness that the needle provided?

"How are you?" Carlton's voice was soft like a night breeze.

"Dead."

"Mrs. Morgan is cooking breakfast."

"I can't eat, especially bacon. Mama made it every day. I can't."

There was a long silence. "Best not dwell on the past too much. Mrs. Morgan cared enough to come cook. You got to eat."

"I'll try." She stood on shaky legs and saw an old dress of her mama's spread out on the end of the bed. The scent of Mama, soaked into the cloth, enveloped Bess as she slid the dress over her head. Carlton gave her a nod.

Mrs. Morgan wore an apron around her rather large stomach. "You're up. Good. I made you some breakfast."

Bess pulled out a chair and smiled at Carlton as he walked through the kitchen and out the door.

"Carlton will be back later."

Mrs. Morgan rolled her eyes and shook her head like Mama did when she was aggravated with something Bess said. "Eat up. You won't starve around here no matter what."

"You was good to Mama before she died."

"Poor little thing. Just bones. You know she was always a beauty and smart as a whip. She loved your daddy better than life itself. I'll never understand her marrying that other one."

Bess accepted the heavy cloak of darkness weighing on her shoulders.

Too Young 1995

"Tell me, young lady, what do you know about Bess when she left here?" The sheriff pushed his dark-rimmed glasses up his nose.

"The state took me away from Bess for neglect and physical abuse. We lived in Asheville. She was seventeen, and I was two."

"She left just as she turned fifteen." The sheriff wrote something in his notebook.

"She was a teen mother." The young woman dug into her purse.

"Some things are just best left in the past."

"I have to know about her."

Betrayal 1978

The first two years Bess lived on the farm, Carlton was there most of the time. He rarely left her alone. He watched as she made a garden and began to cook healthy meals. Each morning she lay in bed and listened to the birds. She didn't allow her mind to go backwards. Her life wasn't perfect, but it was better than it had been. Sometimes, she woke to Carlton sitting beside the bed, watching her as if he expected her to confess to some crime. When neighbors came to call, which they often did, she explained Carlton's presence and their friendship, but most only shook their heads as if she had made the wrong decision allowing Carlton to be there. They refused to speak to him.

One day Red Connor showed up with fresh corn from his daddy's field. Bess told him how Carlton had turned her life around. Red looked at her like she was turned inside out crazy.

He pulled her to him. "What you need is a good screwing, Bess. That'll put him out of your mind. He ain't never done nothing but cause trouble for you."

Bess didn't put up a fight when Red led her down the hall to the bedroom. Nor did she make a sound when he undressed her. As he pumped her full of him, Carlton came to stand in the door. His face like a still lake at midnight, smooth as a plate of glass. When it was over, Bess cried. Without even meaning to, she had betrayed Carlton, the one person who helped her.

Red came every week, sometimes twice a week.

Soon after Red's visits began, Bess cornered Carlton in the kitchen. "Will you marry me?"

The muscles in his face tensed. "Some things are best just left alone."

"It's because of Red." Tears slid down her cheeks.

"Lord, Bess, you don't love me. You don't know everything. If you did, well, that would change things between us. Leave the arrangement as it is."

The wind left her lungs and numbness worked through her heart. Carlton walked away.

To Know You 1995

"I want to know how Bess died even if it was natural causes. What about the man that brought her home?" The young woman pulled a yellowing paper from her purse. Bess, sitting on her perch, stretched her wings and craned her neck; the paper was a letter she wrote years earlier.

The sheriff frowned. "How do you know about him?"

"Bess sent this letter to the state." She pushed the paper at the sheriff. "It begs to know where I am. It tells of a man named Carlton Weehunt that brought her home and saved her life from an overdose. I'd like to talk to him. He might tell me something about Bess."

Thou Shall Not Kill 1980

It was cold and snowing the night Carlton left her forever. Had she known what would happen, she would have changed the story. But some things can't be altered. Bess had turned into an old woman, shriveled from the inside out. Red had been with her earlier in the afternoon. It was his habit to come on Tuesdays. His wife had a weekly Bible study. Carlton stood in the door. Bess had grown accustomed to his odd behavior, needed it, and enjoyed both men's presences. Later that evening as the snow began to fall heavy, Bess made supper. She had long stopped cooking for Carlton, who never bothered to eat. He took his meals elsewhere.

"You wrote a letter to the state?" His eyes showed a seriousness unlike any other time.

"Yes. I want my girl back."

"Leave well enough alone."

"I can't. She's part of me. There is a hole in my heart."

"Our child."

"Have you gone around the bend? No, my child."

He came so close to her face, she should have felt his breath. "It's time to remember."

A hum as loud as a thousand bumblebees sounded in her head. "No."

"Yes. Remember the night you left here?"

Bess shook her head. "No."

"It's okay, Bess. You can handle the memory now. You need to remember." His eyes were deep black. "You put an end to the evil in your life. You got strong."

"Go. Leave now." Anger raced through Bess, cracking the dark places in her mind.

"Right here in this kitchen."

Bess placed her hands over her ears, but still she could hear him.

"You wanted to protect the child inside you."

"Shut up."

"No one was here to see you kill. You covered up the deed and left this farm forever."

Bess threw her plate of food at Carlton but missed.

"Don't you even remember your stepdaddy?"

"Go!" Her scream bounced around the room.

Carlton turned without a word and left the house, walking through the snow, leaving no footprints.

Later that week, Red came. Bess sent him away for good. She cooked. Food gave her a deep pleasure. A plate of cookies took the panic that threatened to swallow her. Cake took away the pain like the drugs once did. She ate. Her body became large, slow, and unhealthy. Still, she could see the look on Carlton's face when he told her the truth.

Into The Sun 1995

"I want to know where I can find Mr. Weehunt." The young woman patted together red lips. Bess had forgotten Carlton's face. But now she looked a pretty version of the man she killed. Bess's heart filled with lightness.

"No one has seen Carlton Weehunt in years. I can tell you he never brought Bess here cause he was missing."

"If I could find him, he could tell me about his years with Bess. He could tell me what kind of woman she was."

The sheriff looked at the young woman. "You see. There ain't no way Carlton rescued Bess from dying. It's some crazy tale she told when she came walking home. Wasn't no one with her, but she sure did insist he was there. Folks up here overlook their own people's oddities. They looked the other way when it came to Bess. Carlton was Bess's stepfather. Disappeared when she did. No one saw him again. Can't say what happened, but, if she was smart, and Bess was smarter than most, she would have put him six feet under. Nothing but bad news, that one."

A rush of cold air blew over Bess. She spread her wings and looked at the young woman, looked her in the eye, as she pushed off the branch. Her beautiful daughter, her heart, her hope, had grown into a woman. Bess was afforded a chance to see her. The wingspread was huge for an inky black crow. Bess sailed through the sky, a shadow on the sun. An understanding wove into each twist and turn her flight took. Acceptance entwined within her soul like a thick golden braid. Sorrow fell away.

The young woman watched the bird until it flew straight into the sun and vanished.

God's Will

by Jon Sokol

Willie Elrod checked his Hav-a-Hart rodent trap in the back pasture. A monster field rat the size of a football lay trembling in the wire cage. "Jiminy Christmas, you're a big one." He knelt down and stared into the black eyes. The rat hissed. "Shush, baby," the man whispered. "I'm not going to hurt you."

He poked a stick into the trap and the rat gaped open its mouth wide, baring cruel yellow teeth. "That's a nice boy," Willie said. "You're going to be okay now. Let's see . . . I think I'll name you Sampson."

He opened a burlap fertilizer sack and placed the trap inside. In a quick, practiced motion he opened the door of the cage, dumped the rat, pulled out the trap, and closed the bag. He twisted the top of the sack and tied it in a loose granny knot. The rat thrashed inside.

"Settle down now, honey." Willie set the bag beside him on the fresh-mowed, deeply pungent alfalfa. "We'll go home soon," he said to the bag. He took off his cap and wiped the sweat from his brow with the sleeve of his flannel shirt.

Still on his knees, he reached for his pink Barbie knapsack. It had belonged to a child he once knew who had very much looked like the blue-eyed, golden-haired angel smiling up at him from the satchel. He unzipped the knapsack and pulled out a sleeve of Girl Scout Thin Mints, a plastic bottle of Pepsi, and a small can of Fancy Feast. He peeled back the cat food lid and snapped it off the can. He licked the bottom of the lid and put it inside the Barbie bag before positioning the can in the back of the cage and setting the trap door.

Willie sat cross-legged in the warm Georgia sun and prayed in silence. After several minutes, his eyes snapped open and he tore into the bag of melting chocolate cookies. He ate until they were gone, taking a drink between each one. He fed the plastic bag into the empty Pepsi bottle and screwed on the cap before placing it back inside the bookbag. Willie then stood up with popping knees, picked up both bags, and walked across the pasture to the barbed wire fence that separated the hay farm from his house.

The farm had once belonged to his father. The two men had lived together in the house for all of Willie's fifty years. After the old man died from a tragic snake bite a few years ago, Willie sold all the land and farm equipment and kept the home, which allowed him to finally quit his job at the sawmill.

Willie had killed his mother, but he hadn't meant to. She died in the downstairs bedroom, paying for her sin while giving birth to him. Willie's father homeschooled him in Old Testament tradition and forbade him to socialize with other children who he said were immoral. Other than work and sporadic trips to Maryville for supplies, Willie spoke to very few people. He liked it that way.

The world was full of sin, and he thought it best to steer clear of others. Because he lived way out in the country, it was easy to do. His closest neighbors were miles away. He saw no one other than the mailman or an occasional Jehovah's Witness. He prayed nightly that

God's Will

God would send the deluge again to drown the wicked that infested the earth. They were no longer worth saving, he thought. Better they should perish than spread their filth any further. *Tell me, Father, how I can help you fight this evil.*

Willie walked into the house through the back door, which opened into the kitchen. He set the backpack on the wooden counter by the sink and hung his cap on a nail. The flies were getting bad. He made a mental note to buy a can or two of Raid the next time he drove to town.

He carried the burlap bag down to the cool musty basement, closed the heavy door, and clicked on the overhead fluorescent lights, careful not to step on the vast throng of rats scurrying across the hard-packed red clay floor.

Against one wall were a number of small cages made of chicken wire, which held several half-starved rats and possums. The rats, he knew, would last three or four days between feedings. The possums, he learned, could last a little while longer. He poured Sampson into one of the empty cages. With a piece of chalk, he wrote on a small blackboard mounted on the wall *Sampson-I*. At the top of the list, he erased the *III* by Abraham's name and opened one of the other cages.

The rat looked up at Willie then walked out gingerly before scampering to the middle of the room where the remains of a naked corpse lay chained to a large eye bolt secured in the floor. The face was nearly gone, exposing greasy, dimwitted skull. A possum was feeding inside the open stomach cavity, its lolling tail the only thing visible. Willie pinched his nose to shut out the sinful odor.

He remembered how hard it had been to drug the young man. Like a good Latter-Day Saint, the stranger had politely declined a cup of coffee—sweetened with sugar and Ketamine—after Willie had invited him inside to discuss the delusions of the Mormon cult. He had been forced to go old school on the boy with ether and a dish rag. The ensuing struggle reminded Willie that he wasn't as young as he once was.

I'll send them to Hell one at a time if need be.

He poured water into several aluminum pie plates before clicking off the lights and walking back upstairs. He sat in a rocking chair in the front parlor, put on his father's reading glasses, and opened up a moldy copy of *Highlights Magazine.*

Outside on the dirt county road, a car drove past the driveway. It stopped in a cloud of dust and backed up to the mailbox. The lady read the name on the mailbox and flipped through several pages in her spiral notebook. She placed a red check mark by one of the names and drove up to the two-story farmhouse. She fixed a blank census form to her clipboard, slid out of the car, and walked up to the front porch, swatting flies along the way.

Cold Canaries

by Kristen Reid

There's a reason they call it the portal of the mine. It's like a one-way trip into another plane of existence that is not for the faint of heart nor for men wishing to remain on the side of the living. Down there, in the unforgiving depths of darkness, a man teeters on both sides with one foot hanging over the edge of life while the Devil tries to greedily grasp it with boney claws. It's an occupational hazard—a formality of daily drawls in this day and age for a bit of bread on the table.

Babcock's sole purpose of existence in West Virginia at the time was as an insignificant, gimcrack mining town that held the prize jewel of Red Hollow No. 2 Mine within its mountainside. It was like a dark monster of fire raging in the midst of civilization waiting to be fed its next batch of flesh when the dawn called for men to ride the tracks deep inside its jaws while sweethearts, wives, and children prayed to it for mercy that they might once again see the faces of the ones they held dear. After months of continual labor with the ever-present loss of men to black lungs or equipment mishaps, the lasting crew members of Red Hollow No. 2 had delved into the mountainside deeper than expected as coal seams became more and more abundant. Each passing day revealed new, uncharted territory underground, thus making the mine a large cavity of numerous tunnels that felt long and copious as if a small village existed under the earth just for the tonnage men to live in. Their 10-hour days felt like continuous night as they rose for the workday in the creeping hours of early morning when the sun had not yet accepted the coming of day. At nightfall, the miners would return home—the sun having long ago departed the sky. The men never knew it as a familiar occurrence but more so as an unseen specter that disappeared as soon as their dust-covered faces emerged from the mine to blend amongst the blackening night as equals.

It was late November of 1906 when the crew had struck something more than coal seams and new passageways leading to the hopeless promise of much-needed earnings and higher wages. What they had cracked open was unwanted and of something that had wished to remain hidden within the walls of Red Hollow No. 2.

While working the mine, the large tonnage crew usually broke off into factions of a sort—factions where men had found kinship with one another and formed alliances underground—so, every shift began with each of them migrating to work alongside a preferred member in the tight rooms. One of these merged groups consisted of Hiram Wickes, Jeremiah "Lizard" Rowe, Elam Barlow, Abner Johnson, and a young boy of fourteen named Benjamin Ladd. The odd family of miners always detached from the main group as a derelict, makeshift clan varying in size, age, and colorful personalities.

"Ol' Lizard's got the run of it like always. Look at him," Hiram grumbled to Benjamin as the stoic man in front of them picked away at a seam with great precision and agility. He always pulled in more tons than the others, dishing out the brass checks with his name plastered onto it to attach to the carts, symbolizing to the pit bosses of his success and reminding them of the competitive pay. "I swear, he's a workin' fool like no other. A timeworn man like me don't much have that kind of fire anymore. Oy, Lizard!" The diligent man turned to regard them both with a straight, flat face without emotion. "You save some for us." Lizard just turned back around and resumed his efforts.

Lizard was mute, or at least he hadn't spoken a word to any soul since he had joined the crew months ago. He had adopted the nickname after only a few days down in the mine once the men had all watched in astonishment at the way that the muscled bloke was able to slink his way between the roof and floor with ease like he was made of rubber instead of bones. Benjamin didn't care for him. He found the peculiar man's reticence unnerving. He wasn't even quite sure which of the group had adopted him as one of their own. He just assumed Lizard had forced his way in with his usual daunting glare being too much to argue with.

Hiram, he liked, though the man was more so a bottle of whiskey or hooch than an actual person. He could drink everyone under the table, and Benjamin would watch him during his benders in unadorned confusion, unable to grasp how such a foul drink—the kind that the men had forced onto himself too many times than he liked to remember—could take over a man's senses and desires to the point that he would continuously clamor for such vile, bottled-up poison. It was Hiram's sleepy stupor and placid eyes that made Benjamin feel calm while he was blanketed in the thick, black grime he slogged during the day.

Abner was his second favored of the men—a moral compass and bright light that shined more radiant than any lamp knitted into their caps. He kept them all sane, singing songs and whistling sprightly tunes to carry them through the disheartening hours. Benjamin hadn't a father for as long as he could remember, and sometimes he wondered if it was because he had been born straight from the coal beds since it was all his mind held onto for memories. He had always placed Abner in that paternal position, and he felt that Abner had assumed the role happily, as the caring man always kept the fears bubbling inside Benjamin at a manageable level whenever the boy flew out of his mind. Elam, on the other hand—

"I heard it coming down this way from the others. All them mules up front . . . they're dead!" Elam exclaimed, hunched over since the roof met the floor too closely for any of the men to stand upright. He raised his darkened arms in exasperation as he continued his fevered statements. "Deader'n doornails, but here's the curious bit . . . they ain't got blood in 'em. How's that to yas? No cuts or sickness held them animals. They was strong. Now they up there laying out on the floor sucked dry, just limp flesh stretched over bone. Don't figure we'll have an easy time pullin' the carts 'til they get new ones in here." Elam sauntered over with his pick slung heavily over his shoulder as he studied Benjamin, who averted his eyes and focused on meddling with a lantern. The rest of the men ignored Elam's reports, keeping their hands busy with work. "What you think, little feller? Think there's monsters in these here mountains? You a brave enough man to go trottin' down those tunnels in the dark and take a look? Huh?" Elam chuckled deeply before lunging at Benjamin. Benjamin swung his fists at Elam, but the older man locked him in a tight hold while Benjamin kept his feet kicking away in hopes of freeing himself.

"Piss off, Elam, eh?" Abner shouted from the room he was working in. "Get on with you, you fool."

Elam let Benjamin go with a sigh and then a smack on the shoulder. "Best be keepin' your eyes out, boy." He left and descended into the room with Abner, and Benjamin could hear the two men pick up in conversation that reverberated out into the tunnel as muffled chatter.

Just as he was getting ready to join Hiram in his labor, an odd flash of something caught his eye down in the pit of the tunnel.

Benjamin walked past the rooms alone, picking up the lantern in his hands and coughing forcefully as his lungs filled with the essence of mine dust and poisoned air. As he walked, he held out a hand in front of himself against the pitch black of the tunnel that stretched on. He could hardly see his hand, as the soot that covered it masked his skin and blended it into the walls of the mine. He only walked enough into the carved depths until it got too tight for him to do so happily and Abner's whistles became not as clear as he would like. As he returned to the men and went into Hiram's room, he caught sight of the same strange apparition he had seen, but this time it ran quickly past the rooms in the direction of the portal.

"Hiram, did you see that?" Benjamin asked, lifting the lantern in an attempt to light the tunnel and view it better. Hiram huffed quizzically, eyes drooping. Benjamin shook his head and started aiding the man by carrying the coal deposits back to the cart. Benjamin looked around for Lizard, wondering if *he* had been the bizarre sight rushing by, but the man was still on his knees chipping away at his area unbothered.

"Get out! Get out!" a man's voice came calling from the portal so far from their area that the shouts almost sounded like faint whispers. "Hurry!"

Benjamin dropped the coal from his arms and raced back to Hiram, poking his head into the room and relaying the information. He did the same to Abner, Elam, and Lizard before grabbing up the lantern to light their way. All the men came bustling out together not knowing fully what the shouts of warning had been in reference to, but they hardly questioned it after hearing all the horrors of nearby mine disasters that were surely not too far ahead of Red Hollow No. 2.

Fear played over Elam's features as Hiram remained his indolent self. Abner held his countenance strongly, and Lizard moved around on his feet quickly like a ghost flying past them all.

With what felt like an eternity of running through the tunnel with their bodies bent in on themselves in the close confines, it appeared that the mine kept stretching on and on longer than it should have. No light pierced the distance to bring them relief in seeing the portal. No sounds of the other men working filled the depths. The silence of the mine was deafening alongside the heavy breathing of the gang and the scraping of their boots clamoring for an exit from unknown demise. The mine never opened up further past the continual cramped space. Abner stopped running and examined the walls in confusion. The others left him behind and kept running, but Benjamin fell back with Abner, who was now bouncing his eyes back and forth between the direction of the exit and the direction of which they had all come from.

"We should've been out of here already. Where's the rest of the crew? Where are the other rooms? The tracks?" he asked with his lungs heaving and a wheeze punctuating each question. Benjamin could hear the huffs of struggling lungs petering out into numbing silence as Elam, Lizard, and Hiram became distant, darkened images in the black mine. "Somethin' ain't right."

There were no rooms attached to the tunnel now. The two of them were solely surrounded by endless coal walls on either side. After a few minutes of inquiries between each other, Abner and Benjamin turned their heads back towards the direction where they had all been working. They could hear boots meeting the rocky floor and shouts of fear coming upon them quickly that way, and Benjamin reckoned it was more of the tonnage company following behind. As the sounds became loud and within a few feet of them, Abner and Benjamin again met the sharp eyes of Elam, Hiram, and Lizard poking out of their black grime masks. All the men looked at each other in confusion with their eyes wide.

"How did yous two get in front of us?" Hiram asked with congested lungs.

"*In front of you?* We've been standing here the whole time! How'd y'all come back from that way? It's a straight shot to the opening! Ain't no circles in here."

"We been runnin' straight! Where are all the rest of them fellers?" Elam threw his hands around in a fury, gesturing at the intact walls. As they stood in the quiet mine, asking each other questions in fearful glances instead of words, the distant sound of whistling echoed in the pits. Two more voices joined in on the haunting, disembodied whistles from afar, and the men all turned to regard the noises coming from the direction of which their rooms were.

"Why'd someone shout to leave if they's all back in their still workin'?" Elam asked before turning to Benjamin in a rage. "You're the one says they told us to retreat. You playin' a game with us, boy? I'll cut your ears off, you little pig," he said through clenched teeth.

"Someone shouted to retreat! I heard it!" Benjamin held up his hands and shook his head, coughing violently and hunching over from the force of it. He hacked up whatever was in his lungs and spit out an odd substance from his mouth.

"Looks like you's got black lungs, boy."

"Shut up, Elam," Abner warned as he listened to the growing volume of the whistles. "I'd like to not be down here if it's firedamp, boys. Burning alive just ain't the way *I* wanna go. Go on, Hiram, and head down that way to see what the rest of them are still doing down there and if all's clear. Elam, you go with him."

"I'd much rather take Lizard. At least I won't die from *his* bluster," Hiram joshed as he met Elam's narrowed eyes. The two men descended the mine with Hiram's cap lighting up the way in front of them. Soon, their bodies were hidden by the darkness again while Elam, Abner, and Benjamin stood against the body-hugging walls awaiting an answer and praying that ruin did not lie in wait for them.

The whistles all joined into a song then instead of haphazard bits of noise, and they grew louder and louder. A bird chirp reverberated throughout the tunnel and merged with the whistles as an equal in the verse of whatever melody they were all partaking in.

"Hear that? That's the canary," Elam whispered, pointing a finger up at the roof. "It ain't firedamp or the air, then, if he's a'warblin'."

"It's gotta be some of the crew. I'm gonna go look," Abner said.

Benjamin shot his eyes to Elam who grumbled, "Oh, so now I guess I'm the babysittin' dolt!"

"Stay here and wait to see if Hiram and Lizard come back."

Elam slumped against the wall and Benjamin followed suit. They sat without speaking as the whistles soon dissolved into silence again—the only sound around them being the creaking of the roof.

Quick footsteps came running up to them from the direction of where the mine portal should have been. Benjamin and Elam jumped up in their spot as much as they could under the low roof as Lizard came into view under Elam's cap lantern. His eyes were huge, and his mouth hung open as his arms flailed about wildly and his knees shook.

"What is it?" Elam asked, his face contorted with uneasiness. Lizard tried to answer with overstressed movements in his lips and teeth, but Elam and Benjamin hardly understood anything that he did. Lizard mimed actions then, grabbing his own throat and making slicing motions around his head before delving into reenactments of what could only be deciphered as a wild man eating. Finally, in the last effort of conveying his message, Lizard tried whistling the tune that they had all heard in the tunnels. A cracking noise came from his mouth as he continued making vicious carving motions around his head and neck. "Damn loony. I knew you was always a creepy little feller, Lizard." Benjamin brushed Elam out of the way and walked up closer to Lizard. The man continued his performance, pleading with his eyes.

"Has someone been killed?" Lizard nodded and motioned between the three of them. "Where's Hiram? Oh, it isn't Hiram, now, is it?" Lizard lowered his head and raked a hand through his messy hair and nodded. Benjamin shook his head in disbelief, thoroughly muddled over the idea, and wished that Lizard could speak. His watered eyes caught sight of something watching them from afar behind a heap of slag in the distance. He turned his lantern in the direction of the thing, and, in just the right angle, two sets of white, beady eyes glowed as soon as the light was cast on them. He saw matted hair and two pairs of long arms bent around the slag mound, and, as Benjamin shouted over to the figures, wondering if they were perhaps stray tonnage men, he watched as both bodies cracked their bones in skewed positions before quickly whistling and descending into the pit further while the sound of clacking hooves marked their retreat. Benjamin howled in horror and dropped the lantern, shattering it to bits and encasing them all in complete darkness save Elam's cap lamp.

"The hell did you do, huh? What is it?" Elam shouted, rage filling his voice as he turned to Benjamin.

"There are things down here with us, and they ain't men."

"You scared now, that it? The dark getting to ya? Maybe it's them things ate those mules up," Elam snickered as he licked his lips and made slurping noises for added effect. Lizard motioned down the tunnel where the things had been behind the slag and made muffled, cautionary noises as he backed up into a wall and slumped down with his knees pulled to his chest.

Benjamin stewed on Elam's comment and then looked back at Lizard. "Just might be."

"Where's Abner? Hiram?" Elam shouted with frustration.

"Lizard said Hiram—"

"Yeah, yeah, I ain't believin' a nutty outburst from someone can't even say the name 'Hiram' with his own tongue. Let's all go back down together'n look. Maybe they went back to the rooms and are workin'."

"Then where's the rest of the men? The opening?" Benjamin asked frantically as he scanned the area in search of what he had seen, praying that it had all been a trick of the light or a hallucination brought on from being emerged in poison air for too long.

"Why don't you shut that hole in your face and come on, then?" Elam pushed Benjamin forward to lead them as he and Lizard fell in behind. They walked slowly back down into the depths of the mine, past the slag heap that had shielded their bizarre stalkers from full sight. It was an endless hall of rock with the promise of pitch-black void awaiting them.

"Makes not a lick'a sense. Feels like it just keeps damn well repeating over 'n over again. Any of this look familiar to ya? It's like the mine keeps shiftin' on us like a maze!" Elam shook his head as he dragged his fingers against the ever-presently close roof. Benjamin's knees ached from being bent for so long, and his neck burned with nerve pain from its constant folded position to keep his head from raking against the rock surface above.

"Hey, what's that there?" Elam asked with a hushed voice. He moved his head so that his cap lantern shown onto the foreign object laying on the floor that they had just come upon. "Holy Mother Mary!"

Hiram's body laid there like an empty substance—a husk of flesh without blood running in the veins. He looked more a skeleton with skin stretched across his bones than a human as his eye sockets were now hollow recesses, and his mouth remained opened from his attempt at screaming.

"He looks like them mules!" Elam whined with panic as he grasped his mouth closed with a shaky hand. All three of them studied the body without speaking. Lizard slinked away from them and resumed his position with his knees to his chest on the floor, whistling the haunting melody of the mine. Elam started screaming with hopeless pleas, calling for their rescue, for someone to hear of their plight, to be saved, but Benjamin knew all too well that miners couldn't expect salvation. The bosses would just find new sops to fill their boots tomorrow when they would all be found dead. To them, there wasn't such a thing as paying for the safety of men when they were as expendable as leaves falling from the trees in autumn.

Hell seemed close to them, and Benjamin lifted his prayers to God, but he knew that God would never turn His ears towards Babcock to listen. It seemed He hardly even remembered creating the bit of land with His powers, abandoning it for demons to run free in its stead. When the Lord called for there to be light in the world, He surely ignored that mining town when He spoke, for light was something to be had for those that were still living with souls rather than haggard bodies that more or less resembled corpses instead of miners.

"We thought we been digging for coal, but it's our own graves we been digging," Elam whispered to himself. "Where the hell is Abner?!" he screamed then as he pounded a fist against the harsh side of the mine. "Abner?!"

Abner's voice came calling then from deep in the pits ahead of them all. It was frantic and full of something demanding and unfamiliar each time his cries echoed in the tunnel. The men fell into line together, running as best as they could towards the voice with their knees nearly rubbing against their chests. Elam and Benjamin both yelled the man's name multiple times, trying to gauge where he was, but the closer they felt that they had come to running into Abner, the farther his voice became.

"Wait. Where's Lizard? He was right with us. He—" Benjamin's voice cracked as he turned his eyes back onto the empty path behind him and Elam. "Stop!" he shouted as he grabbed Elam's arm forcefully to halt the lanky man in his tracks. "Lizard is gone!"

"Not like he could've told any of us anyhow he was leavin'." Elam tried to brandish his snide remarks like usual as if to keep himself sane in the midst of chaos, but as he studied the empty tunnel and looked at Benjamin's gaunt face that held an unspoken burden, he shook his head. "You don't think—"

The idea of what had earlier become of Hiram stabbed Benjamin and Elam's hearts when their thoughts turned to Lizard. Surely it was only their heavily poisoned minds filled with paranoia and hallucinations down in the mine making them all feel like they had lost their heads. Surely there was nothing to run from other than firedamp down there. Surely what Benjamin had seen had not pulled Lizard from their side without a single bit of a cry for help allowed to escape the vulnerable man. Elam and Benjamin stared at each other in horror at the thought of Lizard's soundless begging deaf on their ears. Whatever dwelled amongst them all had enacted unknown sins while the two of them had run away into the tunnel from Lizard without any knowledge as to what was happening mere feet from them.

"I ain't lookin' back, boy," Elam whispered with his eyes unblinking.

"Elam?" Abner's voice called from the pits again, and Elam took off frantically towards it. Benjamin scrambled behind the man to stay in the range of his lantern cap. "Elam!"

"I'm comin', friend!"

"You're running too fast, Elam! Wait! Wait! Please! I can't see! Please! PLEASE! I don't want to lose my eyes!" Benjamin's scream was so guttural and feral that he hardly recognized his voice in its utterance, and it shook his being to the core. Elam's figure became hardly recognizable in the dark. It seemed that the very winds of hell carried his feet further and further away from Benjamin without a second thought. As Benjamin clawed his fingers into the near walls to help propel himself further towards Elam, Benjamin's foot slid on an incline in the floor and his body crashed onto the rigid, cold ground, smashing his head for good measure.

When he finally pulled his head from the floor, he felt the side of it sodden with something wet. As he reached a quivering hand to his temple to determine if it was mine drippings or something more sinister, his fingers stuck to it more so than they would with water, and his stomach turned. He couldn't tell how badly he had been cut, as his hand, when held out in front of himself, was unable to be seen at all to reveal the amount of blood on it now. As he stood, he felt dizzy with pain as his eyes tried to focus on his surroundings. There was not a thing for them to adjust on. There was only a vacuum of black surrounding Benjamin. There was only void.

Benjamin reached his hands out on either side of himself to touch the mine walls and to get a grasp on which way to proceed in the tunnel. He could scarcely make a noise, as the thought of crying, or even being able to have any emotion at all at that point of terror, escaped him. He tottered through the tunnel, unable to rationalize which way to go, but the act of continuing was more so a means to have a purpose than anything else.

The whistling started to echo ahead, this time like a choir of violins that scraped together, untuned in a fit of fury. Benjamin's mind ran freely, reflecting on images of the creatures he had seen. With every unsteady step he took, he nearly screamed with the horror of what might be existing mere inches away from his face, unseen without a light. In an attempt to appease these fears, Benjamin reached out a hand from the wall to feel out in front of himself so that it would alert him to whatever was lurking there, giving him enough time to pray for his soul. Benjamin's stumbling boots met a barricade in the path that had just enough give to it to let him know that it wasn't anything made of rock or slag. It was a body.

The boy wailed as he gingerly stepped over whoever lied beneath him. He could only guess it was Abner or Elam without a lantern to reveal their familiar appearances nestled alongside sunken skin and carved-out eye sockets.

The whistles grew in their ferocity, and the voice called to him from what seemed every direction at that point. Benjamin swiveled in place, reaching out his hands to feel around himself, asking God or whoever would listen to direct his feet towards salvation.

"Benjamin!" The voice screamed through the tunnels like a solo performance amidst the deafening whistle song. "Benjamin!"

His head struck something as he walked blindly, and after contemplating what it had been, Benjamin reached his trembling hands up above himself towards the roof. His fingers met a cage swinging above. He didn't hear the chirping of the canary. He didn't hear any life inside its confines. As he reached inside the opening of it, wishing for a warm, feathered body to touch his fingers, for another life to give him comfort in that mine abyss that robbed him of sight, his fingers clutched instead around a cold little bird.

Benjamin held the dead canary to his chest as he continued walking in the tunnel, the whistles and clacking of hooves both following behind him and awaiting his presence ahead. The boy fell to the floor then and crawled his way in the mine, the roof having closed in tighter and the thought of walking or merely having the energy to stand on his feet being too much for him. He started singing a song to the little bird, one Abner had once chanted during a shift, as he reached his empty hand out in front to pull himself forward against the stiff floor. A fit of hacking and coughs tore his lungs to ribbons and he spit to the side, wishing that his afflictions could take him asunder faster than what he ran from.

"Benjamin! Elam! GET OUT!" the distant voice screeched, but this time it was Abner's. This time it was drowning in pain and torment. Benjamin kept singing. At every angle, the poor boy felt the presence of unseen spirits dancing around his ransacked body, be that the creatures of Red Hollow No. 2 or the ghosts of the tonnage men, he knew not. With an outstretched hand grasping the floor of the mine, praying for an escape from the numbing, black existence he was forever caged in, his coal-dust fingers felt a hard object of what he could only imagine was an animal's hoof and the spindly hair that fell beside it. But Benjamin dared not look up, for he feared that he would see white eyes in the unforgiving black mine.

He would no longer sing, having been robbed of his lungs like the cold canary in his grip, but, like his fellow crew members of Red Hollow No. 2, the boy would linger without his eyes.

CABIN 28

by Emma Cariello

This wasn't pain. Pain was a stubbed toe, hangnail, scraped knee. There was no word for the rotten cavity of white hot burning running quickly across her chest. She heard a jagged, primal screech and startled before realizing with faint, woozy wonder that it had come out of her own mouth. Darkness crept in at the edges of her vision, and she fell into it gratefully. It was cold and hard. It held her in its arms as she fell asleep.

The cicadas were loud that Summer, defiantly so. Anyone who ventured out of their cabin to sit on the porch for some peace and quiet would immediately be driven back in again by the constant buzz. But to the kids splashing in the tepid black lake, the sound was just another track on their summer album. When they stumbled inside, onto spongy floors into the smell of humid, swelling wood, they would miss the cicadas. Inside it was too quiet.

Her son, sunburnt and dehydrated, was sitting beside her. *Oh*, he thought. *Oh*. Refusing to look at her. He was young, but he knew that if he looked at her, he would never get a moment's sleep again. He didn't look, but he listened. He couldn't clamp his sweating hands over his eyes and ears at the same time, and just letting his eyes flutter closed didn't feel like enough of a buffer against the red hot splash of energy next to him.

So he listened, and he heard.

His mother's scream shook the walls, vibrated in his head. Louder and louder, his brain humming with the frequency, her throat raw and still working, time stopping. Louder, louder, until it stopped dead and seconds continued to pass by. The man with the knife huffed. Her mouth gurgled uselessly, as if there was just one scream left that couldn't escape. Her son thought that was the saddest sound in the world and proceeded to vomit into his own lap. He finally opened his eyes.

The TV droned on. They hadn't had time to snap it off when the man with the knife entered. A laugh track chuckled at her son, and he watched pieces of regurgitated hot dog float by.

While the kids floated effortlessly in the lake, their parents chatted and grilled under the pines. The heat was terrible that year, they said. Gas prices were asinine. Fathers shimmying their cargo shorts further up on their protruding stomachs, mothers with flitting, nervous eyes. Always glancing at the small moving dots of their children in the water, then back to the thick woods. They hovered at the edge of those woods, safe in the sunlight and fluffy green grass, in their cozy cabins. They acted as a barrier between the swimming children and that endless ocean of swaying trees, miles and miles of darkness that none of them even hoped to understand. The vacationers didn't want to know what was in there, but they were sure it was much worse than cicadas. At night, their barrier disappeared. The woods crept into their backyards.

The man with the knife dropped his weapon with shaking hands into a deep hole in the backyard where the woods crept. He patiently washed his hands and watched the watery red swirl down the rusty drain in the quaint kitchen, pictures of her son stuck to the fridge. In the living room the two hollow chests rattled together, as if in conversation. Eyes open wide to the ceiling, chatting away about this or that with the thin, shaky sound. He sat between them, drifting off to sleep. Listening to their back and forth, eavesdropping on the newly dead.

INTERMISSION:

DEATH AT WEDDINGS

A Poem by Bonnie Medford
Inspired by Jeff Clemmons

You always wanted a black wedding.
An abbey with a gothic chapel, long roads
through the cemetery. Getting married;
surrounded by the dead.

I watch them filing into the abbey.
I watch you pacing and smiling,
in your black on black tuxedo.

The bride is going to wear all black,
I hear someone whisper as she walks by.

Bonnie Medford

I had planned on formal white.
There was never a black gilded envelope
with my name on it. I spy from the tombstones.
I lean on a marble angel. She's blackened by age
and time has been unkind.
Nothing stops you from smiling, today.

I've seen you very different.
Crying out in pain. Years ago,
we drove to North Carolina.
It began to rain. We began to slide.
The car turned twice.
Glass cracked all over the floor.
I could see you bleeding.

We were both sure you would die
in the mud, with the rain soaking
your face.

You are holding her hands.
Holding them in your hands.
As if she might run away
if you loosen your grip.
I watch you from the tombstones.

I still wear your ring.

The worms let me keep it.

Death Don't Kiss

by Lincoln Reed

In a deft swoop, Sheryl downed the libation and wiped her mouth, grinning in a way that made me forget I was there to kill her.

The lady bartender winked. "This is our yearly date night, isn't it?"

I waved a hand, offering her to partake with me. She nodded her thanks, moved a strand of brown hair behind her ear, and filled another shot. The liquor poured evenly, settling at the top of the glass with precision. "We got a live band coming. Why don't you ease the brakes, sleep it off, and swing by later, yeah?"

Sleep? I didn't know how.

"Just beer today? No bourbon?"

With a curt bow, I sipped my can of Rainier and cleared my throat. "Variety. The spice of life."

"That gives it all its flavor." Sheryl downed her shot. "William Cowper."

"Eighteenth century English poet. A real piece of work."

"Never took you for a man of lyricism."

"That's what they teach you in college? Lyri-cis . . . hmm."

The slurred speech was for Sheryl's sake. She didn't need to know that spiritual entities couldn't get drunk. Her hazel eyes met mine, and, for a moment, I lost my train of thought. Sheryl had a way of getting people to open up and confess their secrets, which I envied, but I didn't hold a grudge against her. I couldn't imagine a man who would.

"In undergrad we studied poetry," she continued. "Liberal arts and all that. A well-rounded education. Sticks with you. Some of it, at least."

"Thought you were an animal lover."

Sheryl wagged her head. "Psychology."

"Waste of money and time."

"Like what you're doing right now?"

Sheryl bit her lip seductively. And if I were a mere mortal, it might have worked. Ambient country music played in the background, sappy enough to make me believe I'd entered into a love song myself.

"Been working here three years," she said with a casual flip of her wrist and a *devil may care* swagger. "Most folks haven't noticed *you*, being a rarity. But I do. Was there the night you first walked through the door, covered in dirt. No car. Drank top shelf until the FBI hauled you away. And, still, a year later, you came back to this little bar in a no-name Wyoming town . . . on that *same* day." Her head turned to the side. "Took me a while since then, but I've finally figured you out. Don't worry. Your secret is safe with me."

"Pray tell."

She shrugged. "For a while, I thought you were a serial killer. Then I changed my mind since nobody around here died when you visited—and the FBI sure as heck let you walk free. You were probably just a guy looking to get laid. Some local would nibble, yeah? I mean . . ." She motioned toward my three-piece suit and head of hair. "Who wouldn't? But you never hung around long. Plus, you're too good looking to be in here without a special *friend*, if you don't mind my saying so."

"I don't."

"Well, I aim to know my patrons, but you'd never give your moniker, not until I asked for ID. You're from out of state. West Virginia."

"Almost heaven."

"Rupert Hauerglaus." She smirked. "Fakest name I ever heard."

"Pronounced *hour glass*. Symbolic of fate. Mine especially."

Sheryl's eyebrows crinkled. "So, *Hourglass,* you're a man who wears a thousand-dollar suit and sips cheap beer in a rural Wyoming bar once a year. Here's what I don't get. You drink here less than a full day, and you tip more than I make in a month with the local crowd."

"And?"

"With money like yours, I had hoped you were proposing a casual friendship."

I lowered my beverage, a bit annoyed. Sheryl was literally flirting with death—a gal at least 8,000 years younger than myself and beautiful enough to have a string of suitors. She could do better, or at least find a partner who wouldn't put a bullet through her head.

The establishment's mounted animal heads, quiet TVs, and silent wall art all had the right idea. Drinking at the Blue Dragon Bar and Grill was supposed to be a silent matter. Why couldn't Sheryl understand that?

"But you don't cat-call, grab-ass, or make any cues," the bartender continued. "If anything, you tip well for reasons all your own."

Sheryl put on a mock expression similar to those I had seen from investigators in TV crime shows. "The current theory is . . . you're anniversary drinking. Washing away bad memories."

"Dragnet."

"Excuse me?"

"Your new name. And it ain't a crime what I do, Ms. Detective. Let sleeping dogs lie, hm? Or call the fuzz. I don't owe anything but the bill and a nice tip. Though I'm reconsidering the latter."

Sheryl glanced around the bar's empty interior. The usual crowd would show up soon enough. For now, I alone sat at the counter.

"Want to talk about it?" she asked, prying with easy eyes and a welcoming demeanor. Her pretty face made a pouty expression. "I'm dying to know."

I should have paid my bill and walked out. But Sheryl was bored, pretty, and the alcohol would be an easy excuse for what I was about to tell her next. With mental wheels spinning, I tried to rationalize why it would be okay to breach protocol. Sheryl wouldn't believe my story. Nobody would. But this specific assignment was three years overdue, and I was losing resolve.

"Hey, Rupe. Earth to Rupe."

Sheryl hadn't moved.

I had nowhere to be. No appointments, commitments, or targets waiting. Just Sheryl.

What could it hurt? She was going to die anyway.

"Never told a living s-soul this." I took another glug. "But it's true. All of it."

Sheryl sashayed around the corner of the bar, walked to where I was sitting, pulled up a stool, and poured herself another shot of whiskey. Lounging beside me as any decent drinking confidant would, she drank the liquor and motioned for me to continue.

"Tell it straight. From the beginning."

We don't have enough time for that.

I sighed, checked my watch, and considered if I should use a knife, gun, or my hands.

"You know those pill commercials?" I asked, talking slow, easing into a steady reveal. "The cheesy pharmaceutical promos with smiling actors, minimal health benefits, and an endless catalogue of gruesome side effects? That's me. A laundry list of bad omens. The endgame every physician and pill pusher is paid to help you avoid."

"What a bad boy."

"And, like those pills, I've been working up a cure for my patients. Slowly, sure. In one particular case, though, I've been delaying. Procrastinating. I've offed thugs, gang bangers, mafia crooks, corrupt politicians, and even the occasional drug cartel. They deserved it. All of them. But not this one. It doesn't feel right snuffing her out."

"Whoa, whoa, whoa." Sheryl's body tensed, her voice lowering to a whisper. "You're a hitman?"

"Bounty hunter. A debt collector."

"Explains the suit. But not rural Wyoming."

"Dress for the job you want."

"So, you're legit then? A real boogieman?"

I swirled the beer in its can, contemplating why I was bothering with an explanation. It felt good to share my secret, even if it was with someone destined to perish by my gun.

It's decided. I'll use a gun. Make it quick.

I paused for a beat, building the anticipation for what I'd disclose next.

"I'm fallen. An angel of death in human form. But I can't return to paradise. I'm cursed. Eternal damnation. That's what I'm due. No redemption. Made a choice long ago to side with Lucifer, the Morning Star. Regretted it ever since. In recent centuries, I've been trying to prove myself worthy to the Almighty, taking assignments from governments and agencies, destroying evil people, terrorists, criminals, and regimes. I've worked with the FBI, CIA, NSA, and Homeland Security. They give me a list of names. A quota. In return, I boost my resume of 'righteousness.' But it's not simple. America isn't all good. And they're not my only clients."

"Whatever you're smoking, I want some."

The empty aluminum Rainier crumpled in my fist. "Then I met you."

"Right. Three years ago today. Got it. All caught up."

"I hesitated. Drank my fill and walked out the door. Didn't do my job."

Sheryl frowned, clearly taken aback. In an instant her sarcastic leer vanished, replaced by a pale expression. Hers was a familiar reaction, but one I never grew used to.

"I've never . . . not one as milk-toast as you," I continued. "So, I've been delaying. Watching. Stalking. Studying."

She was listening, hanging on every word.

"Took my time with your case," I said, releasing the can, letting it rattle on the bar top. "Yours is a slow death."

The doors squeaked open. New customers entered the establishment and joined me at the bar, sitting on the far side. All were loggers, dressed in flannels or work coats, donning dirty boots and unkempt beards—stereotypes one and all, cursing and jabbing each other with sharp tongues. A few gave me a quick look, perhaps wondering what a man dressed like the Wolf of Wall Street was doing in their favorite watering hole.

Sheryl rose from her seat and straightened her black tank top. With trembling hands, she brushed bangs from out of her moist eyes and donned a smile to hide trembling lips.

"Still want to hear my story?" I asked.

The bartender turned and walked around to the other side of the bar. She poured tap beer for the newcomers, casting fleeting glances in my direction, overpouring the liquid above the pint glasses, hands shaking as she placed the beverages on the wooden bar.

"You okay, Sher?" asked one logger.

"Who's the suit?" said another, pointing in my direction.

Sheryl leaned forward and whispered. The loggers seemed amused at first, but when Sheryl didn't break, they turned serious. One told her to call the cops. Another volunteered to "end me."

"Just long enough, would you?" she murmured lower than any mortal would be able to hear. I perceived her voice clearly. "Till the cops come?"

Logger number one, whom I chose to name "Larry," patted "Moe" on the shoulder and nodded for "Curly" to follow suit. The fourth stooge remained where he sat at the bar, the oldest of the flannelled white knights and wise enough to know I'd get to him on my own time.

Larry, their leader, strode forward with Curly and Moe in the rear. He rolled up his sleeves and casually gave a macho up-down with his eyes.

As a being first formed in the spiritual realm, a few perks came with the territory, including the ability to perceive the inner workings of the human psyche. As such, I instinctively knew that Larry was an egomaniac while Moe and Curly were obsessed with beer, porn, and cigarettes—in other words, weak willed. Should Larry fall, his two compatriots would flutter like leaves in the wind.

"Howdy," Larry said, arms crossed.

I unceremoniously swiveled on the stool and faced my visitors.

"Where you from?" asked Moe.

South of heaven, north of hell. Nowhere in between.

"Can I buy you boys a drink?" I asked.

"Sheryl says you're being weird," continued Larry. "Acting the fool."

I grinned. "White, aren't they?"

Larry flinched. Moe frowned.

"My teeth. Pearls, yes?"

Larry glanced at his wingmen, puzzled.

"You know, the thing about teeth is, they're not a medical necessity. Purely cosmetic. But that's how you judge someone, isn't it? Straight, clean teeth means a healthy body, someone who takes care of himself, a person of means and responsibility."

The stooges watched as my grin widened.

"And then, when death nears, teeth loosen. Fall out. But you still live on, sure. Dentures. Fake chompers. Day after day, year in and out, you look in the mirror, not paying attention to the ticking clock, wasting precious seconds flossing and brushing until . . . ." The Glock 19 nine-millimeter raised in my hand. "The Debt Collector taps you on the shoulder and says *time's up.*"

The three stooges backed away with hands raised and eyes wide. I stood with the gun centered on Larry, allowing the grin to fade into my usual tight-lipped expression. In my right hand I held the Glock, and on my left wrist I checked a gold watch, counting down the seconds.

"Listen, mister. Didn't mean no harm. Just protecting Sheryl."

"Oh, I know." I studied the aged watch's second hand make its way toward the 12. "You three have a chunk of years left."

I glared at each man directly.

"Larry, you've got seven, maybe eight, winters if you stop smoking. Cancer's a nasty bloke. He cheats me in golf every weekend, but he won't shortchange you. And, Moe. Oh, lascivious Moe. Enjoy the ride, my friend. The rollercoaster ends in another five summers. Curly? Sweet, lovable Curly. Be nicer to your wife. I won't be as forgiving in three years."

Larry's fingers tightened into a fist. "Only cowards gun down unarmed men."

"Of that, we can agree."

The Glock reentered its holster within my suit jacket.

"Besides," I said, studying the watch, "I'm not here for *you*."

Larry and company observed as I counted down, "Five, four, three . . . ."

Across the bar, sipping his beer, the eldest logger grabbed his left arm, wheezing. I raised my right hand, still looking at the watch.

"Two, one . . . ."

When my fingers snapped, the fourth stooge collapsed onto the floor. Larry, Moe, and Curly cried out, ran back to their friend, lifted his head off the floor, and felt for a pulse.

Widowmaker. I licked my lips. *Rupert Widowmaker. I like the sound of that.*

By the time the stooges rallied for vengeance, I was gone and so was Sheryl. She'd slipped out the back door during my little demonstration.

Outside the bar, I walked down the street and disappeared into an alleyway, winding my watch back another 24 hours, counting down the seconds until Sheryl would beg for her life.

My fake hangover lasted a full day.

I "slept it off" in a small RV rental hitched to a diesel truck parked at the local camping grounds within walking distance of the Blue Dragon. Forest and mountains surrounded the quaint Wyoming village, but I wouldn't stay to hike or hunt.

Bang. Bang.

I checked my watch. *Right on time.*

Bang. Bang. Bang.

"All right!" I called, imitating the vocal inflections of a North American rural delinquent. "Let me get my pants on."

I rolled out of the bunk, pretended to crash onto the floor, cursed, fumbled for a light, and flipped a switch. What could have been a pristine RV living space was in fact a thriving civilization of empty beer cans, snack bags, and dirty clothes that littered the kitchenette and fold-out table. I might have spared the owner if he'd kept his unit clean.

The knocking paused long enough for me to find a pair of workable jeans and leather boots. I tugged both on and zipped the fly with an ostentatious burp worthy of an Oscar.

Bang. Bang. Bang.

I swore with the same tone and inflection as the RV's late titleholder.

The door swung open, allowing brisk fall air to cut through the threshold and liven the RV's musky interior. With breath pluming, I raised my hand to block the morning glare. When my eyes adjusted, I beheld a small lady wearing what could be best described as expedition gear. She was decked out in hiking boots, pants, a camouflaged coat, and her reddish-brunette hair was tied in a ponytail underneath a thick sock hat. It took only a moment for me to recognize the visitor's face.

She extended a gloved hand. "Hiyah."

"You're early."

"I'm biting the bullet."

"Sheryl . . . please," I said with a country drawl. "No puns."

"Eliza," she corrected. "Eliza Monarch. Sheryl's a pseudonym. Keeps the bar creeps away, you know?"

"How's that working out?"

She dug into her coat pocket and revealed a wad of cash money bound by a rubber band. "I'm hiring your services."

Without having used basic mental math since the time of Noah when all one had to worry about was counting forty days and nights, I tried to register how much dough Eliza was offering. It couldn't be much. The stack appeared to be a horde of small dollar bills.

"Tips from the past three years. Been saving for school. And since the pandemic cuts erased my PhD research funding, I've got to pay my way through." She extended the cash. "But now I'm cashing out. There's a guy in town who's going to kill me. And I can't trust the police."

I slammed the door and the RV went dark again. The fresh mountain air lingered for a few seconds before losing the battle to a stench of unwashed clothes and old fish sticks. I sat on the bed and massaged my mask with a thumb and forefinger, relishing how well my disguise was working.

Bang. Bang.

"Callaway, listen. I hid the big bills between the small ones. It'll be worth your time."

I threw open the door again, now pointing the Glock at the shocked expression of a startled graduate student. Slowly, I removed Calloway's skinned face off my own.

"Pay me off? No. Once a price is on your head, the hit can't be undone."

Eliza's jaw moved but no words came out. Gradually, she started dry heaving and then bent over and puked. I waited, steadying the handgun, seething as I wiped the dead man's grime off my cheeks. I sneered. "People like you, the goody-two-shoes who *think* you're righteous . . . you make the job unbearable."

"Where's Bob Calloway?" her voice trembled as she stood, body frozen like a statue.

I shrugged. "Where he belongs. Sex offenders have a special suite down below."

Her nose scrunched. "Had no idea."

"If you're going to hire a hitman, maybe do a background check."

I could sense the gears turning in her head, plotting, figuring a way she could avoid the inevitable. Finally she broke, resorting to what some humans do when faced with immense stress—humor.

"Geez," she said. "The layers I could peel off your onion."

Eliza tapped the side of her head, explaining the metaphor and the joke. The tell-tale sign of a poor comedian.

"How about this," she continued. "I pay enough dough so you leave me alone for another year. You'll be the subject of my dissertation . . . ."

"There's plenty of paper and ink in hell."

"But no spell check, right?" She paused, waiting for me to laugh. "C'mon. At least let me die thinking I'm funny."

"Not interested."

"In the money, the dissertation, or me being funny?"

My fingers loosened around the Glock. The wristwatch ticked silently, seconds closer to finally closing the bounty on Eliza Monarch.

"There's got to be a loophole," she continued. "Something I can do to call off the dogs. Rupe, help me out here. What's the fine print?"

"Why?"

"Because I'm a good person! I don't deserve this."

I sighed, still holding the gun aimed between her eyes. "For three years I've watched you, making sure I hadn't made a mistake. And, for a while, you fooled me. The volunteering with special needs kids; donating to charity even though you have little money for your own schooling; and, worse yet, your desire to actually use your skills pro-bono, which would make sense since you're considering a law degree next. The list goes on. Not to mention the years you spent in the Peace Corp.

People like you, the goody-two-shoes . . . that doesn't mean you're exempt. Deep down, everyone's rotten. Even you."

"I want to hear my options. There's always a second door."

"Not with me."

"Who wants me dead?"

"Somebody up the chain of command."

"Does *somebody* have a name? Because if it's Cassie from the university janitorial crew, I'm sorry, okay? Toilets should be able to flush baby wipes."

Her comedic strategy was getting old. "Strike one."

Eliza tapped her chin, thinking. "Lucy Fredricks. Grade six. Hated my guts. Always said she'd put a hex on me. Are those chickens roosting?"

Enough already.

"My boss wants you gone. Erased. Zeroed. Put in a body bag and dropped in the Hudson."

Eliza simpered, processing the threat. "So, if I'm hearing you correctly, you're going to stuff me in a trunk and drive me across the country . . . only to dump me in the dirtiest river in the Western Hemisphere? Just so you can reenact a mafia movie? I'm more of a *Goodfellas* gal myself, but I'm getting *Godfather* vibes from you, Rupe."

"I don't kill horses."

"Fair enough. But tell me this. If the devil wants me dead, it must be because I'm going to do something really noble with my life, right? Like, I'll cure a disease or arrest all of the pedophiles in the world, give all puppies a safe home . . . ."

"That info's beyond my pay grade."

"But you hesitated killing me. Even now you won't pull the trigger."

"I don't enjoy killing women."

"Charming. You've got the looks, too. Considered Hollywood?"

"Not my department."

"Rupe." She wagged her head. "What're we doing here? Why can't you just walk away?"

"Because," I said, breathing slow. "Once I finish this final job, I won't owe Lucifer anything. I'll be free to find redemption."

"And I'm the last name in your little black book?"

I nodded.

"But you never answered my question about fine print."

"You couldn't stomach it."

"Momma said the same thing about ice cream, but turns out I really like sugar. And I've got a hunch you're hiding a few scoops, aren't you?"

The Glock lowered. I leaned against the door. "There's one way, yes. But nobody ever takes it because no one's an idiot."

"All ears."

"To free yourself from the bounty, you must find a third party *willing* to take your place. Doesn't matter who. But blood has to be shed, and it can't be coerced."

Eliza looked at her shoes. "Oh."

"Queasy yet?"

She stuffed the cash back into her coat pocket, shivering in the mountain air. "How long do I have?"

"Two hours."

Eliza rubbed her arms. "And nobody's ever found a replacement?"

"Centuries ago, a buddy of mine was driven out of a man and into a herd of pigs. Stranger things have happened."

"Peachy."

I tapped my wristwatch. Eliza took the cue and returned to her Subaru Forester. The car's model name gave me an idea. I'd bury her in the forest.

Eliza Monarch was doomed.

She knew it.

And I couldn't help but feel sorry for her.

My typical assignment was to kill persons who'd committed heinous crimes, not post-graduate students who possessed humanitarian ideals. Sometimes I'd do dirty deeds for the CIA one day and the next day complete a task for Lucifer himself. For me, it didn't matter who gave the job. I was a willing vessel—a double, even triple, agent. All that mattered was freeing myself from every obligation, debt, and commitment. Then I'd be free to find a possible path to salvation, just like Eliza during the final two hours of her life.

In her situation, most people didn't know who to ask or what to do, and, in many ways, Eliza reacted as all the others had. For the first hour, she sat in her car, perhaps thinking and debating how she could justify asking a complete stranger—or a trusted friend—to sacrifice his or her future for her present safety.

I guzzled coffee from the front steps of the RV, but the caffeine had no effect. All that mattered was the liquid's warmth. It reminded me of paradise and the never-ending love of the Almighty. Hell, for me, was a literal icy pit separated from my Creator—one I didn't favor any more than a needle through the eye. In that sense, I pitied Eliza. I understood her destination, and I didn't desire her fate.

When the first hour had completed, I knocked on her passenger window and offered to ride shotgun, hating myself for the pun. She obliged and we drove throughout the quaint Wyoming town, thankfully avoiding a pitstop at the local church.

The Forester's first stop was outside a lone trailer home at the edge of the village. I remained in the car while Eliza walked to the front step.

She tapped the doorframe, but no one answered.

Next we visited a lady with Alzheimer's, but she proved an unwilling substitute. Eliza returned to the car, more frazzled now and less jovial than she'd been when swapping witty remarks outside of the RV. Reality was settling and making its home in her psyche. Her once pleasant scent had now shifted to what every mammal smelled like when trapped in fight or flight. Her glands gave forth sweat and her eyes fought to keep back tears.

Finally, she came to grips with her task. What did she have to lose? If people thought she was a horrible freak, it wouldn't matter. She was going to die. At least I was giving her a chance. A professional courtesy.

We frequented more locations and persons, allowing Eliza the best opportunity at finding someone who was already contemplating suicide or considering "saint" status, but no one took the bait. Doors slammed in her face. People cursed. Others called her possessed.

Each time she returned to the car, her eyes were more dilated.

I inspected my Glock 19, awaiting the conclusion of Eliza's final three minutes.

She started the car again.

Her expressions morphed and twisted as if her internal struggle was being displayed by every muscle in her face. Then it finally happened. She broke.

"Please! Another hour. We can make the hospital cancer ward and . . . ."

The realization hit before the words left her mouth. Eliza's eyes fell and her bottom lip quivered. Waterworks streamed down her cheeks, but I offered no condolence.

My finger neared the trigger.

"Y-you're right." She sobbed. "I'm horrible . . . for even thinking that . . . wanting it."

I instructed her to switch seats with me. She obeyed.

Now in the driver's seat, I weaved the Forester along mountain logging roads and through dense forests until settling at a scenic overlook that pictured snowy crests and a serene lake.

"What're we doing?" she managed to ask between wiping her nose and drying her eyes.

"Giving you one last glimpse of beauty."

We silently watched the azure, cloudless sky as morning turned to afternoon, observing primal nature in its purest form, basking in the radiance of the Creator's majestic handiwork. When dusk approached and the sky turned fantastic shades of pink and orange, I raised the Glock.

"Wait," she said, holding up a palsying hand. "Where's my kiss?"

I scowled. She patted her lips. "You know, *the kiss of death*."

"Death don't kiss."

She frowned. "Doesn't."

"Exactly."

"No. You said it wrong grammatically. It's 'death *doesn't* kiss.'"

"You're going to fit right in."

"Down below?"

I kissed her hand. "Where else?"

DEATH COMES IN THREES

by Greg Bhatia

Eddie Rollins finally showed up for work. It wasn't like he rushed in—or even strolled in—though he was quite late. One minute he wasn't there and the next minute he was, standing near a pile of rubble. He surveyed the scene of devastation before him, caused by the depredations of the *Luftwaffe* bombers that snuck across the English Channel each night to drop their deadly loads over London.

Oye Eddie, I shouted. *Welcome to the party, mate. If your lordship is done surveying his jurisdiction, perhaps you would care to join us commoners and lend a hand in removing these bodies?* Eddie just stood there looking at us sadly, so Bernie, the foreman, finally said, *Eddie, get your butt over here right now! You think these poor sods will move by themselves, eh?* The entire crew roared with laughter at the grim humor as we stood amongst the stiff corpses of the unlucky victims of last night's raid. The country was in the middle of a war, and the only way one could go on doing this morbid sort of work without going insane was to pretend that the dead were just part of the rubble. Humor was where the crew often found solace during working hours.

Death Comes in Threes

Eddie, however, continued to look at us sadly, which was unusual for two reasons. First, Eddie had always been eager to show up for work, so his tardiness today was out of character. Secondly, Eddie was a bit of a clown with a seemingly bottomless repertoire of jokes and funny anecdotes, so his standing there now with that hangdog look gave the crew some pause. *What's wrong, Eddie?* I asked. Eddie responded by pointing in the direction of some buildings in the distance. *Death comes in threes,* he said. *What did he say?* asked Bernie, then in his sixties and getting a little hard of hearing. *I think he said 'Death comes in threes,' Guv,* I replied. *Now what the heck does that mean?* asked Bernie, frowning. *I have no idea, Guv, but he sure looks sad,* I replied. Bernie turned towards Eddie and said in a gentler tone, *Eddie, come down here, son, and tell us what is bothering you.* Eddie didn't respond and instead started walking off towards the buildings that he had previously pointed to. *Ralph,* said the chief, addressing me, *You better go after him and see what this is all about.* He then commanded, *If this turns out to be one of Eddie's usual pranks, I want you to yank the bugger back by his ears so we can give him a sound thrashing. Roger that, Guv,* I said. I motioned for one of the other lads, a chap called Harry, to come along, and we both took off after Eddie.

We found Eddie standing in front of a building that had been partially destroyed in last night's bombings. While the lower level of the building was still intact, the upper portion had taken a partial hit by a stray bomb. Half of it had been reduced to rubble while the walls of the other half stood precariously, the roof ready to fall down at any moment. I recognized the building immediately and exclaimed, *Christ, Eddie, isn't this where you live?* Eddie nodded sadly while he looked at the building. *Death comes in threes,* he said again. I knew that Eddie had shared a flat with his best friend Mike, Mike's wife (whose name I could not remember), and their two-year-old daughter. *Eddie, were your flat mates at home when this happened?* I asked. Eddie nodded sadly again and pointed towards the now-demolished second level of his building. I felt sorry for Eddie and told him so. *We will find them, Eddie, don't you worry,* I said as we climbed the stairs, which were thankfully still intact, in order to reach Eddie's flat.

The corridor was dark and littered with rubble. Dust hung in the air, barring our way as if in silent protest of the cruel manner in which we humans treat each other. There had been only two flats on the upper level, and only one (presumably Eddie's) had been destroyed. The other had escaped with only minor damage, though it was still unsafe due to the danger of the roof collapsing. Harry and I knocked on the door of the second apartment, which was opened by a wizened old lady in her petticoat. She peered at us across ancient glasses that had seen better days. *Ma'am, this place is not safe anymore, do you have somewhere else to go?* I inquired. She shook her head, so we gently led her downstairs and, after collecting the tenants from the downstairs flat, we took everybody to the building next door. One of its tenants graciously accepted them to wait over tea while we telephoned the fire marshal to come assess the building. *It may be a few hours before the fire marshal makes his way here, sir,* I said to the tenant, a retired colonel of the Royal Fusiliers regiment. *Not an issue, young man,* he said. *Thank you for your service. Thank you for yours, sir!* I replied as Harry and I left to go back to Eddie's flat. There, we found Eddie standing near the door, looking sadly inside.

The flat had once been home to living, breathing human beings, but a cruel twist of fate had reduced it to dust and ashes. We started removing the rubble in one corner of the flat and worked our way around methodically as Eddie stood in the doorway watching us. *Here!* shouted Harry suddenly, and, as I walked over to him, I saw a hand sticking out from beneath the debris. We dug out the body, which turned out to be Mike. I looked over to Eddie, trying to convey my silent condolences, but he kept staring elsewhere. We resumed our search and soon discovered another body, this time of a woman, whom I assumed to be Mike's wife. This left only the child, and the prospect of finding her corpse was not something either Harry or I was looking forward to. Children were difficult, always difficult, and no amount of jokes and grim humor helped with the horror of seeing a little hand or foot sticking out from the rubble. Steeling ourselves, we resumed our search.

I had just cleared a large section of the wall that had collapsed when I discovered the crib and the child sleeping within it. By some miracle, the wall had collapsed at an angle where it had lodged itself against another wall, thereby sheltering the crib from other debris that had rained down. The child had been trapped in this safe space and must have cried all night before falling asleep from exhaustion. Tears came to my eyes as I stood watching her little chest rise and fall, and, when I turned towards Harry, I could see his eyes wet with moisture, too. Gently picking up the little girl so as not to wake her, I turned towards Eddie and whispered, *She is alive, mate! She is alive! It's a miracle!* Eddie looked at us with a sad smile. *Death comes in threes,* he said again while pointing towards a doorway leading to another room that we had yet to explore. I wondered aloud if there had been other occupants in the flat we didn't know of and told Harry to go look while I cradled the sleeping child in my arms.

Harry must have been digging for a minute or two when suddenly I heard an exclamation and the sound of his falling. I rushed through the doorway and saw Harry kneeling on the floor, unhurt and staring towards the spot where he had been digging, eyes wide open with shock and fright. I walked closer and saw for myself the dead face of one Edward Rollins, known as Eddie to his friends. His broken body was buried between a pile of rubble, even as, somehow, he also stood in the doorway behind me, looking as sad as one can be.

Beneath the Boat

by Austin C. Nichols

With a full tank of gas, John Whitmore guided his father's Chrysler Mariner deep into the Pacific waters, moving further and further away from humanity. He rocked the boat back and forth to lighten the mood. On the horizon, darkened clouds swelled, aching to give way to plundering waves of rainfall. John was determined not to let a little bad weather ruin their day. Three companions, Lilith, John, and Victoria, had snuck away from their parents' home in search of a seaward adventure. Instead of sleeping the night before, John had flipped through his Marvel comics, giddy for the day ahead. More often than not, he found himself gravitating back to the thought of Victoria in a bathing suit. In a sleep-deprived state of unconcern, John failed to acknowledge the dangers involved in aimlessly taking a boat out to sea with a storm brewing in the distance.

Cruising steadily, John hit a wave harder than expected. The boat momentarily skipped like a stone on a pond before falling back into place. Victoria and Lilith laughed and shouted as they enjoyed the roller coaster-like ride. John could barely hear them talking as the wind whistled and twirled around his head. All the while, he guided his father's boat further away from the shore, further away from humanity. He had never felt so cool and in control. Truth be told, this was only the second time he'd ever driven a boat, but he figured it wasn't worth mentioning to his friends.

When the boat slowed to a halt, there was no visible land in any direction. John slid out of his seat and maneuvered to the stern, where Victoria met him with leaps of excitement. In the meantime, Lilith stared into the distance, overwhelmed by the vastness of the sea. She hated the feeling of being surrounded by the seemingly infinite body of water. Victoria's shrill voice caused Lilith to nearly jump from her seat. "I didn't think you had the guts," Victoria said, lightly tracing her finger across John's bare chest. John replied coolly, "My Dad will never find out. I'm not even worried about it. He's such a damn stickler Vic, always neck deep in his work. He took a plane to New York to settle some business. We could even take the boat out tomorrow if we wanted to." Lilith chimed in, "How about we just get through today first. Then, we'll go from there." Victoria's piercing eyes darted in her direction as she mouthed, "You promised." Lilith shrugged and whispered back, "Sorry." *I'll ease up*, Lilith thought. *I promised her I would relax.*

Together they danced, listening to "Big Shot" by Billy Joel, singing along to every word. John cracked open a brew and, with infatuation flooding her senses, Victoria followed suit. In the meantime, Lilith sipped a coca cola, watching as the two love birds swooned. She had no interest in drunkery; her father's alcoholism had turned her away from the bottle. "No, not for me. Not now, not ever," she'd say. John and Victoria knew not to ask. Instead of drinking or swimming, Lilith flipped open a Shirley Jackson novel. Meanwhile, the sun's rays were growing increasingly hot, drawing John and Victoria into the water.

Within ten minutes, Lilith was immersed in her novel, delving deep into its pages. Reading was her escape from the harsh, sharpened edges of reality and, just like the darkened waters, the words began lapping within her mind. Lilith waited and waited, patient as the hours ticked by. When midafternoon arrived, the sky began to glow a sickly yellow color. Lilith felt nauseated and contemplated asking John to take them back to the boatyard, but she promised Victoria that she wouldn't be the Debbie Downer. Sunlight no longer penetrated the dark, salty waves, which seemed to laugh as they splashed against the side of the boat. An eerie stillness lingered in the air, a stillness that only Lilith could feel. John climbed back into the boat for a moment, asking Lilith if she was okay, but before she could respond he grabbed the boat keys, stuck them in his pocket, and cannonballed back into the abyss.

Let them have their fun, Lilith thought. *Surely we'll be leaving soon.* In the midst of counting her breaths, Lilith closed her eyes, drifting off sweetly into a dream, a land of peace far away from the nightmare brewing below. Meanwhile, John held Victoria close as their legs lightly treaded the water, sending vibrations deep beneath the surface. The creature twitched, sensing a disturbance. Colossal eyes creaked open for the first time in centuries. The creature's awakening reminded it of how long it had been at rest, and an intense feeling of hunger erupted across its massive frame. Unbeknownst to the three friends above, the primalistic mass expanded its fins and thrust itself towards the boat. From the deepest, darkest crevice of the ocean the creature arose.It floated upwards slowly and methodically, intending to satisfy its appetite. . Victoria felt a thrust, a scaly thud of great proportions. John's smile suddenly vanished. He coughed once and threw his head backwards. His body's last response was a great expulsion of blood, which splattered across Victoria's face. The creature's jaws had taken only a snippet—a mere taste—and the creature had found him rather delicious.

John's wretched, death-laden screams pierced the air, tearing Lilith from a peaceful dream and submerging her in a nightmare. Her eyes, bluer than the morning sky, took in the crimson-painted water and the gory scene nearby. The upper half of John's body floated beside the boat. His lower half was absent, only ragged skin left where his pelvis should have been. The creature vanished beneath the boat momentarily, aching for another taste. An insatiable hunger guided its primeval movements as it glided back to the surface, barreling towards Victoria.

With wild strokes, Victoria frantically made her way to the boat's ladder, but little did it matter, for the creature snapped off her left leg and tore the other to shreds. Lilith grabbed Victoria by her wrists and struggled to pull her closer. When she finally managed to pull Victoria aboard, Lilith failed to notice her friend's pale, lifeless gaze. Frantic droplets blurred Lilith's vision as blood poured uncontrollably from the gaping holes in Victoria's body. In a state of shock, Lilith screamed, "Stay with me Victoria! It's going to be okay!" Lilith could barely catch her breath, desperate to help her friend. Sobbing, Lilith screamed, "I can stop the bleeding, I can stop the bleeding!" Frantically, she grabbed a beach towel, remembering what her gym teacher Mrs. Self taught her sophomore year in health class, and began applying useless pressure.

Lilith's body trembled, shaking uncontrollably. The iron aroma of death masked the air. In the water, John's body vanished with a "plop." The creature's stealthy movements pulled its colossal frame out of sight, but Lilith saw what it was. Nothing she had ever learned about sea creatures prepared for a monster of such proportions.

Victoria's body rested upon the stern, slumped in an eternal slumber. Blood soaked into the boat's carpet, spilling over the side and into the water. Lilith's heart thundered against her chest as she glanced off the side of the boat and into the water. Her mouth hung partially open—the face someone makes in response to a jump scare in a scary movie. A "thump, thump, thump" pulsated within her ears. Lilith whispered to herself, "This has to be a nightmare, please God let this be a nightmare." The words barely escaped her mouth. Panicked, she reeled around and reached for the boat's ignition. *No key.* Suddenly, a black supposition dawned over her being, snuffing out what was left of her rationality. *No. God, please, God, no.* Nobody was near, nobody knew where they were. Thoughts dashed inadvertently across her mind. *Where the hell are the boat keys?* Had she told her father where she was going when she left the house? Would he even be awake from his drunken stupor? The whole of humankind was an unfathomable distance away, mocking Lilith lost at sea.

Dour clouds crowded overhead, shadowing the day, preparing the sky for more rain. In that moment, Lilith noticed, or more so felt, that the boat had been drifting. Fat droplets plopped down on her face, falling in line with her tears. Lightning rippled across the sky as Lilith curled into a ball on the boat's blood-stained floor.

BETTER BOY

by Juliet Rose

The way the glob of tomato pulp with a seed sticking out bobbed up and down every time he chewed and swallowed made her want to vomit. Yet, she couldn't stop staring at it. Up and down, up and down.

"We are doing our best, Kate. You know that right?" His question snapped her out of staring at the glob, and she met his eyes.

"So you say. I just don't understand why there has been no info. Nothing. It's been over a year."

He shifted uncomfortably in his chair, making the sunlight bounce off of his sheriff's badge. It almost made her laugh. It looked like the toy badges they would wear as kids while chasing each other around the yard. She always wanted to be the bad guy, her sister the cop. Seemed fitting at the time. She enjoyed being on that end of the chase.

It had been over a year since her husband's disappearance. Fifteen months and seventeen days to be precise. It had been a sunny, cold early spring day. Nothing out of the ordinary. Nothing that morning when she climbed out of bed for a hot cup of coffee made her think everything would change.

They had been together going on fifteen years. Started out typical for a small town. They met through her sister, through a friend of a friend at a house party. Choices in the small town were slim, and they both liked each other alright. He was smart and sometimes funny, she was clever and sarcastic. They laughed, went to shows, and screwed. By the time a year rolled around, it only made sense they should make it permanent. They had a small ceremony, his brother and mother came, her parents and sister were in attendance as well. Small town wedding. Pretty ordinary.

A few years later, his mother passed and then her father. Both by cancer. His father had passed long before they ever met. Her mother moved into the local nursing home not wanting to be on the farm anymore. Her sister wanted no part of the farm, so Kate and her husband moved in. Ready to start a family. But the kids never came. She brought up adoption a couple of times, but he wasn't interested. Flesh and blood and all that. So they got dogs and a cat. And she grew a garden. He worked a town over at the plant, middle-level management. She worked part time at the bookstore. Books became her company.

Over the years they drifted apart. They still screwed every couple of weeks and told themselves that proved they still loved each other. And they probably did in a way. They watched the same tv shows and laughed. But she noticed when they talked he often was just looking past her at his own reflection in whatever glass or mirror was around. She suspected he had cheated but honestly didn't care. Sometimes she wished he would just run off with whoever he was sticking it to. Just let her go. But he never did. He always came home. She flirted here and there with customers but had no energy to pursue anything anyhow. It always ended with mediocre sex and obligatory conversations she was tired of having. She much preferred being by herself with her books and her animals. They never made her feel like shit.

"Kate? You still with me?" The Sheriff reached out and touched her hand. She had known Mike since they were kids. He was a couple of years older than her, maybe the same age as her sister. She thought maybe he and her sister had even gone to a dance or two back in the day. Like a lot of kids in the town he stuck around, taking care of aging parents. He became Sheriff, one of the few decent-paying jobs in town.

"Sorry, Mike, thinking about the garden. Need to get out there and weed it, ya know?"

"Sure, sure. Quite a green thumb you have. These tomatoes are the best I have ever had. I appreciate the sandwich and coffee. You didn't make yourself a tomato sandwich?"

Ugh, she really wished he hadn't said tomato as it drew her attention back to the glob. Her stomach churned and flipped.

"No, I really wore myself out on them to be honest. Luckily, I can sell them in a basket at the bookstore and they go fast. I haven't had one in ages."

She hadn't had one in fifteen months and seventeen days.

It had been a sunny and cold early spring day. She had spent the morning tending to her vegetable seedlings in the greenhouse. It was her favorite place to be. When it was quiet, the dogs would usually come and lay at her feet. The cat would get up on the shelf and talk at her. He would never come in, and she liked that fine. It was her space, her time. Her stomach started to grumble, and she realized she had skipped breakfast. She petted the cat and headed towards the house to grab a bite.

He was sitting at the table reading the paper. She scooted past him and started digging through the fridge to make a tomato sandwich.

"You hungry?" she offered.

"No. I ate." He didn't look up from the paper.

She hated the way he spoke to her now. It wasn't cruel, but it was always with a touch of disdain. Like he felt he was better than her. As if his existence was a favor to her. When she tried to make conversation, he responded with an air of arrogance. So she quit trying for the most part except to find out when she could be alone again.

"So, you have plans for today? Going anywhere?" She hoped she didn't sound too eager.

He sighed, put the paper down, and stared at her. "Why, Kate? Trying to get rid of me?"

He said it like he was trying to be funny, but his irritation came through. Her face flushed, and she turned away. Why did he have to be such a dick? She grabbed a knife and started slicing tomatoes. How the hell did she end up here? As a kid she decided she was going to get out of this town and do things. Be someone. Fourteen years and some odd months later here she was, stuck in the same crappy show. No way out. This was it until one of them died. Tears pricked her eyes. Fuck, fuck, fuck. She didn't want him to know he had driven her to this. Flashes of light started behind her eyes. Her ears started ringing.

He sighed irritated again, and she snapped. She walked over behind him. As usual he ignored her as if she were a ghost in her own home. She stared at the balding patch on the top of his head, grabbed his forehead, and slit his throat. She expected him to fight, to resist. But it was almost as if she put him out of his misery. Out of hers. He sat for a few seconds, blood gurgling out of his neck, and then slumped forward. It was too easy. Almost comical.

She sat down on the couch and just stared at the coffee table. It didn't really happen, right? It was one of the television fantasy reels where the character looks up and nothing actually happened, it was all in their head. They shake their heads and go on with their normal day. She glanced over at the table. Nope. He was still dead. Fuck.

She slowly got up and made her way to the kitchen. She had to move past him again. She half expected him to jump and grab her and take her down with him. But he stayed slumped over. She washed her hands in the sink and tried to think. What now?

Hours passed. She sat on the couch and ate her tomato sandwich. She had to do something soon. It was getting late. She went to the greenhouse and grabbed a shovel. The dogs were playing with each other out in the yard. The cat, who had been snoozing on the shelf of the greenhouse, opened her eyes and gave a crackly meow.

Kate went to the garden and started digging. She felt like eyes were on her, and she kept replaying her story in her head. Oh, you know, getting the soil turned, about to plant the seedlings. Hope it won't frost again. Easy laughter. Oh, he headed to town to grab some things. You know men, just can't sit still. Roll of the eyes. Nothing out of the ordinary.

But no one ever came. No one ever questioned. The hardest part was getting his body to the garden and into the hole she dug. The dogs excitedly trotted along as she pulled him on a tarp, acting like they wanted to help. Once he was buried, she planted the vegetable seedlings on top just like she would any other year. Just planting the garden. The dogs knew after years of being chased away with the shovel not to dig up the garden. It was just too easy. She drove his car into town and walked the six miles back out to the farm.

When she returned, she called the police. Really, just a three-man sheriff's department. She was worried he hadn't come home after running errands. If they see him, could they have him call? She waited til the bars closed and called again, this time a little more frantic. She thought maybe he had stopped off for drinks? No, they hadn't argued, she had been working in the garden all day. They said they would keep an eye out and for her to call if he came home.

The next day she called in tears. He hadn't come home, she had fallen asleep on the couch waiting. He hadn't called. They were more concerned and would ask around, reach out to his work. They called later and had found his car parked at the community center, which they said was a little strange and they would follow up on that.

They called later that day. Work hadn't seen him but did have a little juicy detail of a woman he was seeing a town over. They didn't know her name but gave a description. Maybe he had run off with her. Poor Kate, cheating husband, dutiful wife. How could he? The woman was never identified, but everyone assumed they had run off together.

Days passed, then weeks. She kept calling the sheriff's department for any updates. She called his brother, who had moved to Idaho. Had he heard from him? Did he know anything? You know how he is Kate, you are better off without him. And she was. Her life settled into a quiet routine. She ate when and what she wanted. She watched what she wanted. If she woke up in the middle of the night and wanted to blast music, she did. She tended the garden and sold the veggies for extra cash. She moved to full time at the bookstore. She sold her tomatoes in a basket by the register. The whole town was guilty without knowing it.

It was too easy. Fifteen months and seventeen days later, she made her regular call to the sheriff's department. Mike answered and, to her surprise, said he was going to stop out to have a chat. She felt her stomach flip and said she would appreciate it. Why would he come all the way out?

When he pulled in she was bringing in tomatoes from the garden. They waved at each other, and she invited him in.

"Hungry, Mike? I can make you a sandwich and put a pot of coffee on?"

He nodded and followed her in.

They sat in silence for a minute before he cleared his throat.

"I just wanted to come out and speak with you face to face."

The knot loosened in her stomach. Her brain came down from overdrive. He went on. It was time to let go, to move on. It had been too long. No leads. Etc, etc, etc. He ate the sandwich between talking, getting the glob stuck to the corner or his mouth. Finally he sat back and tapped his middle finger on the table.

"Kate, you are a beautiful woman with a lot going for you. I think it's time to let yourself live again. You didn't deserve what happened to you, but what happened, happened. He's gone, doing whatever he is doing. It's time to move on." He reached out again and touched her hand, this time a little too long. She pulled her hand away and handed him a paper napkin, gesturing to his mouth. He blushed and grinned.

"Best tomatoes ever." He wiped his mouth and set the napkin down, the juice from the glob spreading a red circle onto the napkin.

"Better Boy," she murmured, sipping her coffee.

"What's that? The name of the tomato? Ah, damn fine tomato from a damn fine woman." He met her eyes. She looked at him and down at his throat, afraid her eyes would tell. His Adam's apple bobbed up and down.

She stood up and stuck her hand out. "Thank you, Mike, for coming out. I think you are right, I need to let this go. Let me bag up some tomatoes for you to take with you. I know you are busy."

He stood up awkwardly, not missing the brush off. He nodded and put his hat on. He took the bag of tomatoes and smiled, embarrassed. As he headed out the door he turned and watched her for a moment. She was staring out at the garden with a strange look on her face.

"You know, Kate. Sometimes life turns on a dime. Unexpected things happen, and we can't let it define us. It's okay to live."

She glanced at him and nodded. He raised his hand in a wave and left. Once the dust had settled from his car leaving the long drive, she picked up her gardening gloves and headed out to the one place that knew her best.

Flesh and blood and all that.

Torch's Fate

by Ben Meeks

I woke feeling like I'd spent a good night drinking. My head pounded. I kept my eyes shut tight. I could see the light through my eyelids alternating between light and dark. It was coming back to me now. I was a member of the Tortured Occult Motorcycle Club, an outlaw motorcycle gang made up of any kind of shifter big enough to ride a hog. The nice thing about being a werebear was that I was bigger and stronger than most of the other shifters. It came in handy. I groaned in misery. Did the club have a party? That would explain how I was feeling. Last time, I woke up passed out in a ditch on the side of the road. My miserable nostalgia was suddenly interrupted by the gruff voice of a nearby man.

"You don't think it's waking up do you?" the man asked.

"You new guys are so jumpy," another man chided. "They always make noise like that. We have it drugged and strapped down. There's nothing to worry about."

"It looks like a regular guy. Are you sure it's one of them?"

"The tests were conclusive," a third man said from in front of me.

I pretended to be asleep, trying to remember how I got here. My head was slowly clearing. The last thing I remember, I was heading up Interstate 75. I was close to Dalton when I found a crappy hotel to stay at. I was laying low, waiting for some heat to die down. I got a pizza and a six pack. I was just sitting down for a nice night of watching reruns on a fuzzy TV, drinking, and jacking off. Then I woke up wherever the hell *here* was.

I could feel restraints on my arms and legs. They were tight enough that I knew I couldn't slip out of them. At the same time, I had no intention of just going along with whatever they had planned. They had to unstrap me at some point and, when they did, I'd make my move. I peeked an eye open—just a sliver. I was being wheeled down a hallway. Three people were pushing the gurney I was on, but I could see only the one in front of me clearly. He looked like a doctor with a white coat and a clipboard.

They didn't speak again, and I didn't move. They wheeled me into an operating room and put the gurney beside a table. I could feel them loosening the restraints on my left arm and leg. I was hoping they would undo all four, but I felt them starting to put restraints back on my free arm. I reasoned that the gurney was lighter and more movable than the table, so I knew I had to make my move. It was now or never.

My eyes popped open. The man trying to put a restraint around my left foot gasped with surprise and jumped back out of reach. The fear in his eyes told me he was the new guy.

"Hold him down you fool!" the doctor bellowed from somewhere behind me.

One of the men, who I realized was an orderly, latched onto my arm. He couldn't match my strength, so I launched him over me and onto the floor. New guy came forward, and I kicked him hard in the stomach. Clutching his abdomen, he rolled backwards and out of sight. Another of the men, dressed in a lab coat, pulled a syringe from his pocket. He yanked the cap off with his teeth and lunged at me.

I had no intention of letting him stick me with whatever the hell *that* was. I pushed off the operating table in his direction. The gurney shot across the room, plowing into him and dumping me onto the floor. I took the opportunity to unstrap myself before making the change into my werebear form. My body added bulk, black fur sprouted all over my body. Razor-sharp claws emerged from my fingertips, and my feet turned to paws. My head became that of a fierce black bear.

The orderly I had thrown pulled himself to his feet and took out a stun baton. The end crackled with electricity as he pushed the button on the shaft. He thrust it forward at my chest. I jumped to the side, dodging the baton. Grabbing his baton hand, I yanked him towards me. With my other hand, I grabbed him by the back of the neck and slammed him face first into the glass door they had wheeled me in through. He dropped the baton on the first hit. The second left a blood splatter on the splintered glass. He went limp on the third. His body fell to the floor in a heap when I let go.

"Is that the best you pig fucks got?" I shouted.

I shouldn't have stopped to talk. Electric pain shot through my back. The new guy had found some courage and a baton of his own. I convulsed involuntarily until he let go of the button. My legs gave out and I crumpled to the ground next to the gurney, which I pulled over my head to use as a shield.

"What do we do?" the new guy shouted.

"Keep shocking him," the doctor commanded.

I had a good view of the new guy's legs from under the gurney. I swung at his ankles and knocked him to the ground. Grabbing his shirt, I pulled him in and bit his head. He started to scream and thrash around on the floor as I increased the pressure from my jaws. The baton snapped like a bug zapper as he flailed around. His skull began to snap, crackle, and pop like a bowl of Rice Krispies and then gave way. His body went limp as my jaws clamped shut. My mouth filled with blood and brain matter that felt silky on my tongue. I spit out what I could as I tossed the gurney to the side.

I stood up to find the doctor picking up a corded phone mounted on the wall in the corner. I took two steps towards him and raked my claws across his face. He collapsed face down, a puddle of blood running out onto the floor around him.

They had taken everything I had. Wallet, phone, the buck knife I kept strapped to my boot, even my clothes. All I had on was a bloody hospital gown. I ripped it off, hit the door release, and stepped into the hallway. Outside the operating room, doors lined the hallway. They reminded me of the kind of doors they had in solitary the last time I got locked up. Beside each door was a control panel with lots of buttons and gauges. The hallway continued to the right. I didn't feel them turn the gurney when they rolled me in, so the exit must be straight ahead. I stopped by the first door on the way out for a closer look. I recognized only some of what all the gauges were measuring. Temperature, humidity, O2, and PSI.

I stepped up to the small window in the door and looked inside. The room resembled a plain metal box. No bed, no toilet. It had recessed lighting protected by grates. A woman laid beside a drain in the middle of the floor. She looked Middle Eastern and wore a hospital gown that had fallen open. She didn't seem to care or even notice. Her black hair was tangled and matted. She'd clearly been locked up a while. My last prison cell looked like the MGM Grand compared to this place.

She lifted her head and our eyes met. I could tell she'd given up already. I'd seen the look before. As she turned away and laid her head back on the floor, I heard a thumping coming from behind me. I turned to see a werewolf pounding on the glass in the cell across the hall. I didn't recognize him; he definitely hadn't spent any time at the clubhouse.

Get me out. He mouthed through the glass.

I had a feeling I'd run into more trouble before I made it out. A little help wouldn't hurt. I went over, gave him a nod, and noticed the sprinklers in his cell were on. They covered the entire inside of the cell with constant rain. He looked like he'd never been dry. I scratched my head and looked at the panel beside his cell.

> Temperature: 37° Celsius
> Humidity: 100%
> PSI: 12.5
> O2: 12%

I turned the humidity dial all the way to the right and pushed a button, causing all the lights in the cell to go off. I pushed it again, the lights came back on. I looked back in the cell. The sprinklers had stopped.

Pull the lever. He made a motion with his arm as if he was trying to get a truck driver to blow their horn.

I did see one big lever on the right side of the panel. I gave it a tug and could feel the metal flexing from the pressure, but it didn't move. Surely there was a release. I started pushing buttons all over the panel. The gauges changed, but the lever wouldn't move.

> Temperature: 43° Celsius
> Humidity: 100%
> PSI: 14
> O2: 20%

A wall-mounted alarm complete with red flashing lights sounded. I looked back into the cell to find him still standing by the door, but now steam seemed to be rising up from his body. Back at the panel, I found a red button on the bottom by the lever. I pushed it and felt the lever release. The door swung open and the werewolf stepped out. The hallway filled with hot, humid air.

"How do we get outta here?" I asked.

The wolf shrugged, "How the hell should I know? I'm Atticus by the way."

Two guards ran around the corner. The first collided with Atticus, sending them both tumbling to the floor. The second stepped back and raised a gun in my direction. I grabbed his wrist as he pulled the trigger. Bullets slammed into the wall and ceiling as I twisted his wrist until it popped. I grabbed him by the shirt, slamming him into the wall with as much force as I could muster. His ribs cracked upon impact, and I let him go. His body slid down the wall, coming to rest in a crumpled heap on the floor.

I turned to find Atticus wiping blood from his mouth. He had bitten and ripped out the guard's throat. I turned back to the first. He was still alive and holding onto his gun. I stepped on his hand and ground my foot with my full weight. He screamed as the bones in his hand were crushed. I reached down and picked up the gun from his mangled hand. He clutched his hand to his chest and coughed, blood trickling from his mouth. I pulled the magazine from the gun to find it loaded with silver bullets.

I knelt beside the injured man. "This ain't lookin' good for you. Tell me what I want to know, and I'll think about letting you live. How do we get outta here?"

The guard grimaced in pain. "There are three exits. Your best bet is the tunnel. Go up one floor and turn left. Follow it to the end. You'll find some stairs that will take you out."

"What about guards?" Atticus asked.

"Procedures are to contain the building and wait for help. Everyone will exit and call a team to retake the building. We were trying to get out when we ran into you."

"I believe you," I said.

I stood and kicked him in the chest. The impact forced the air from his lungs, sending blood splattering over my leg. He collapsed onto his side and struggled to breathe. I thought about kicking him again, but I was sure it would kill him. He was barely hanging on as it was and would probably be dead in a couple minutes. No reason he shouldn't spend his last minutes thinking about the mistake of fucking with me.

"What happened to 'thinking about letting him go'?" Atticus asked.

"I thought better of it," I said. "Let's get outta here."

"Hold on," Atticus said. "Let's let everybody out. If they're bringing in backup, we'll need some of our own."

I didn't think we were going to organize this group into some kind of militia, but the more of them there were to shoot at, the better the chance I had to get away. I went to the cell with the woman in it.

"They open like this," I said, pressing the button and pulling the lever.

The door swung open. The woman looked up at me again and laid her head down just like before. I wasn't surprised. I wasn't going to waste my time trying to help a corpse that didn't have the decency to die. I moved down one side of the hallway opening cells while Atticus opened the other side.

What came out of the cells was the sorriest excuse for backup I'd ever seen. There were a bunch of shifters, a goblin, and even a few humans. Most of them were emaciated. They looked sickly and pale. If any one of them had tried to join the Tortured Occult, they would've been laughed out of the clubhouse. But, since all I needed was meat shields, they would do.

What's weirder were their cells. They were all different. Atticus's cell was pouring water, others had bright lights, some were cold. There didn't seem to be any rhyme or reason to it. I saw only a few that seemed normal. Maybe it was some kind of experiment to see how people dealt with prolonged exposure to different conditions. It didn't matter, and I didn't care.

"Anybody that wants to get outta here, follow me," I said, holding up the gun I'd filched off the guard.

We moved quickly and quietly, following the guard's directions up the stairs and down the left hallway. It looked like he'd been telling the truth because the halls were empty. We rounded a corner and came to stairs leading up to a storm cellar door. I grabbed Atticus's arm to put some space between us and the others. I let go as soon as I did when I felt how hot he was. It was as if I had grabbed a radiator.

"Listen, if this whole thing goes sideways and I don't make it out, find a friend of mine named Obie," I said, shaking my hand. "He can help you. He's kind of a big shot in North Georgia. He'll find this place and shut it down. One of those do-gooder types that really annoy me. You hold the left door, I'll get the right. Let them go first," I whispered.

He gave me a side-eyed glance then nodded. He knew what time it was: save your own skin time.

"When we get outside, spread out and move fast. Just get away for now, and we'll figure out what to do next when we're safe. Alright, let's go," I said, pushing the door open.

The door opened into the woods. Atticus and I got a chance to look around while the group shuffled past us. I could see the lights of a large house behind us through the trees, in the same direction as the tunnel. I figured that was where these people had been held. I could hear the rushing of a river off to my right.

The wind changed, and I caught the scent of humans. I couldn't tell exactly how many. I could hear rustling coming from all around us in the trees. As the last of the prisoners moved out past us, I caught Atticus's eye. I gave him a subtle nod in a different direction than the group was moving. We let go of the doors as flood lights illuminated the area.

"Go back to your cells and you won't be hurt," a voice said over a megaphone. "If you attempt to escape, you'll be shot."

The spotlights were arranged in front of us in a half moon shape. It looked like I had a shot of escaping off to my right. Before I could make my move, the goblin with the group made a run for it. The guards had no intention of giving another warning. Guns burst to life, muzzle flashes giving away the positions of the guards. Atticus and I crouched instinctively. Then, Atticus started screaming.

I thought he'd been hit and looked over. Smoke rose from his body before he suddenly burst into flame. It wasn't like he was doused in gas; it was as if he was made of gas. He burned so hot he scorched some of my fur. The air filled with the sickening smells of burning hair and flesh. Atticus took off behind me in the direction of the river, leaving burning footprints on the ground.

I soon realized that most of the prisoners were having bizarre reactions. I didn't see any of them run off, but some had just disappeared. A couple of them dove to the ground and gave up. I moved up and used one of the prostrate shifters as a shield as I returned fire. The guards fired back at me. I could feel the bits of rock coming off him hitting my fur. I managed to shoot out one of the spotlights on my side before my magazine ran out.

Staying there was suicide. I ran into the woods to my right as the stone coyote collapsed. I could see Atticus flailing around in front of me, catching brush and trees on fire as he went. I took two bullets through the gut and fell to the ground. Atticus kept running, screaming and bouncing off trees as he stumbled his way through the woods. I crawled through some brush for cover until I was clear, then got up and moved as fast I could.

I knew I'd been hit with silver. There's a special burn to it you just don't get from lead. When I'd put some distance between myself and the shooting, I leaned up against a tree and inspected my injuries. One bullet had passed clean through while the other was still in my belly. I'd die if I didn't get it out soon. Not knowing where I was, my best bet was to go to a human hospital. If I could find a road, I could get someone to call an ambulance. The club could sort out the rest.

I couldn't very well show up to a human hospital as a werebear. I'd have to change to my human form. Shifting with a silver injury was bad enough, but a silver bullet stuck in my body would do a lot of extra damage. I clenched my jaw and made the change. I could feel my flesh tearing around the bullet. I felt dizzy, but I had to keep moving. I wasn't sure exactly how long I stumbled through the woods before I found a road. I walked into approaching headlights with one hand up and the other holding where I'd been shot. The car slammed on its brakes and came to a stop a few feet away. I stepped forward, put a bloody hand on the hood, and passed out.

"Doctor, he's waking up," a woman said.

I could hear the steady beep of a heart rate monitor and smell disinfectant. I opened my eyes to see a young nurse standing over me.

"Try not to move," she said with a smile. "You were shot and have been unconscious for just over two weeks. I'm glad you're finally awake."

As my head cleared, I saw a man turn around. He was wearing a white coat and holding a chart. He had a bandage over one eye and four claw marks running down his face. I recognized him. My claws had given him those gashes.

"You caused quite a problem," he said as he absently flipped through the pages of the chart. "Yes, you should do nicely."

"What do you want with me?" I asked. "What is this place?"

"A research facility," the man answered. "We study your kind here and conduct experiments."

"What kind of experiments?" I asked.

"My specialty is bioengineering . . . genetics," he said. "There are numerous experts taking part in the experiments, though."

I tried to move but found my arms and legs in restraints. I pulled against them, shook, and screamed but couldn't break free.

"We upgraded our security measures after the trouble you caused. I should really thank you. While you cost us months of work in some cases, we'll be better off for it in the long run. Are we ready?" the man asked the nurse.

"Yes doctor."

"Okay then . . . we'll just take a bit today," he said. He tied a tourniquet around my left arm, just below the shoulder. "We'll use the Gigli saw today."

The nurse handed him a wire with a handle on either end. He

leaned over, inspecting my arm as I struggled. I knew I wasn't going to get loose this time.

"Do try to be still," he said. "I prefer to have a clean cut."

He looped the wire around my arm just below the elbow and gripped the handles firmly. The wire sliced down to the bone on the first pull. Blood, my blood, spilled out on the table. I could feel the wire bite into the bone with the next pull and then the pain hit.

WALKING WITH STRANGERS

by Dawn Major

In 1977, Dandy was five years old and lived in Downey, California. She was the stereotypical California kid—blonde, sun-drenched hair, golden skin, cornflower blue eyes—who piled into a VW bug with her mom and sisters and headed to Long Beach on the weekends. During the week, she rode her pink Barbie bike up and down the same stretch of bleached white sidewalk with a neighbor or parent keeping an eye out. She wasn't allowed to circle the block until she turned six.

After Dandy was born, her parents, like many others, fled Compton to its bordering neighborhoods—to Paramount, Norwalk, and Downey. It wasn't crime ridden where she lived, but not too far from her sidewalk, there were uninhabited houses that were now boarded up to make way for the freeway, and recently the TV had reported news of the Hillside Strangler.

In the mornings, she walked with her older sisters, Gab and Amy, to the end of the street where her sisters boarded buses to go to the middle school, and Dandy joined the elementary school kids to cross the intersection at Dunrobin Avenue and Imperial Highway. The crossing guard ensured the kids got safely across the four lanes to walk the remaining way to Gauldin Elementary. It was a short distance once across, and staff waited outside to usher the children into school.

Dandy repeated the pattern after school. Stop sign lady, traffic halts, children cross, except, this time, the neighbor waited on the other side of Dunrobin to meet her. Her mommy would collect her when she got off work. Tomorrow would be different, though, because the neighbor was out of town. Gab and Amy's school got out later, and Daddy worked second shift this week. Dandy would have to walk home by herself and wait alone inside until Mommy got home.

In the evening before bedtime, Mommy brought Dandy a key and said, "Listen closely. I'm tying a piece of yarn to your key. You're going to wear it under your shirt, but don't play with it or take it off. Got it?"

"Got it. Can I wear it now?"

She wanted the key to hold at night under the covers to protect her from the hummcies—the creatures who lived under her bed and came out when it got dead dark.

"Not now. I'll give it to you in the morning. Come on now. In bed."

Mommy handed her Sunny Bear, walked out, and shut the door.

"Mommy, leave the door open."

Dandy imagined Mommy already gliding down the dark hallway, far away from her, so far away she wouldn't hear Dandy's screams. She yanked her pink coverlet over her head. She must be completely covered or the hummcies would drag her under the bed. Even Sunny Bear wasn't safe and had to be tucked in.

Mommy opened the door to say she wasn't going to leave it open because Daddy watched TV when he got home. It would wake Dandy. "Now, go to sleep."

"*Noooo*, Mommy. I can't without the door open. *Please.*"

"We talked about this already. You're a big girl now. You even have your own key."

"Will you leave the light on?"

"Okay." Mommy turned the light on and off, laughing, on and off, on and off.

"Stawp! Mommy. Stawp!"

Mommy finished her game with the light off and said calmly, "The light isn't good for you."

Neither Dandy nor Mommy spoke for a moment. Dandy watched Mommy, who wordlessly gazed into her room; Dandy hoped her silence meant she changed her mind about the light. When Mommy finally spoke, she said, "You look like a mummy . . . wrapped up in your blankets." Her chuckle sounded far away, and she seemed to laugh at something other than Dandy being a mummy. "What are you afraid of?"

"Hummcies."

When Shelli, the neighbor's daughter, babysat them, Gab and Amy begged her to let them watch scary movies. The homunculi from *Don't Be Afraid of the Dark*—tiny shrunken-headed creatures with hollow eyes who live in total darkness—terrorized Dandy. Shelli told them they fed off souls and preferred children to adults because their souls were juicer, not as corrupt as adults who were carriers of sins. The hummcies took children under the house to do something really, really bad. "They possess your body and steal your soul, taking over your human body, turning you into a homunculus."

"What happens to your human body?" Amy asked.

"It just continues like normal, but instead of your soul there's a demon inside there and the demon makes its human body commit evil acts. They're all over the place, but you wouldn't know it."

Gab asked, "So, how do you know if a person is really possessed?"

"You don't," Shelli said. "They blend in because they look just like you and me. When you've committed all the evil you can in this world, the homunculus come back for you and eat you. That's how the homunculus get stronger. Eventually the whole world will be full of homunculus."

"That doesn't even make sense," Amy said. "Why would the demon let the homunculus eat it?"

"Because it forgets it was once a homunculus. It's just the natural cycle."

"That didn't even happen in the movie," Amy said.

Shelli laughed and said, "So. It's better than the movie."

Gab and Amy didn't believe Shelli; they told Dandy it was make believe, but Dandy had seen them. Dandy couldn't pronounce homunculus, though, so she called them hummcies.

Mommy huffed a little and said, "I've told you before. If it's your time, it's your time. And . . . we don't have a basement, or wherever they come from. Besides, they're not real."

Dandy wanted to trust Mommy, but there was something about the hallway light contrasting against Mommy's body with the darkness coming from Dandy's bedroom. There was something about Mommy that made Dandy not believe her when she said hummcies weren't real. Her silhouette stood stark against the soft light, as if she was absorbing the darkness out of Dandy's room. She smiled, and her once straight teeth that looked like the white Corningware plates they ate off appeared jagged and dirty. Hummcies had nasty, spiky teeth, too. Dandy was afraid Mommy wasn't Mommy, but she put it out of her mind because she loved her. She was the only Mommy she had.

"I'm scared, please, Mommy, *please*."

"Gab's coming in thirty minutes."

Dandy shared a bedroom with her middle sister, who had a

different bedtime than her. They slept in matching twin canopy beds. A small nightstand stood between the beds and held a white glass lamp with the tiniest of pink roses climbing up the base. The shade was white with fuzzy, pink polka dots on it. The same material hung over their skeleton-framed canopy beds.

Mommy walked into the dark room, never turning on the light, pulled a sheer scarf from inside the nightstand drawer, and placed it over the shade. Then, she reached under the shade and flicked on the light. The light seemed to strike at her, though, because she lurched away, protecting her eyes with an open hand.

"Go to sleep."

"What if they come up from the basement?"

"Sweetie, we don't have a basement. Now close your eyes."

She'd seen the crawlspace. The cover to the entrance looked just like the grill over the fireplace in the movie where the hummcies came out. Her eldest sister, Amy, removed the cover one day and told her to look inside. It smelled earthy. Dandy couldn't see all the way to the back of the house. "If you sneak in my room again," Amy threatened, "I'll you lock down here . . . with the hummcies."

Later that night, Dandy awoke in darkness. Someone had turned the lamp off. She yanked her coverlet over her head, but it felt too thin. Anyway, nothing other than light would protect against the hummcies. She strained to hear Gab's breathing, but all she heard was a light hissing. The harder she listened for Gab, the louder the hissing got. She told herself it was Gab's stuffy nose. She stuck some of her coverlet into her ears to stifle the hissing sound she was now certain came from beneath her bed, calling out for her to play.

Dandy was paralyzed by fear. She remained stuck to the mattress even now as the hummcies clawed through the floor, out of the shadowy depths of the crawlspace beneath her bed. They shredded the carpeting with their jagged teeth and thorny nails. She heard them hissphering, *Come with us, come play with us*. First one, then another sprung onto her bed. She felt the slight pressure of their bodies leaping onto her mattress and their spiny legs crawling over her body hidden beneath the coverlet. They reminded her of the time she saw a spider sac burst open and hundreds of baby spiders spilled out. Another pounced. And another. How many? Five, six, eight, ten. She curled into a ball and tucked the quilt tightly around her body to prevent the hummcies from getting under the quilt. Some began to claw. A talon here, a talon there pierced the quilt. She had to get away. Dandy lowered the edge of her quilt just beneath her eyes and found herself staring into the white, glowing eyes of a hummcie. *Come play with us,* it hisspered and grinned a mouthful of glass shards. A line of drool travelled down its dry, crusty lips and landed on the bridge of Dandy's nose. She screamed.

Dandy flung aside her quilt, knocking several hummcies across the room. A thin line of light seeped through the crack at the bottom of her bedroom door, and she recognized the faint sound of the TV. Daddy was watching TV in the living room! Daddy would protect her! Daddy!

Dandy bolted from the bed to the door. She rubbed her hands on the wall near the door, searching for the light switch. The hummcies retreated when she dashed to the door, but not for long. She couldn't find the light switch, gave up, and dropped to the carpet. She stuck her fingers between the door frame and the carpeting, grasping at the only source of light in her dark room. Dandy dragged her hands from the bottom of the door in search of the doorknob. Nothing. One hummcie, then another grabbed hold of both her ankles. They were weak by themselves, but if there were enough of them, they would be able to drag her under her bed, to the crawlspace.

What would they do to her in the damp earth beneath the house? Take her soul? Make her a hummcie? Dandy whined, "Daddy, Daddy," but she was hysterical and choked on his name. She gave up looking for the doorknob and dropped back down on her knees. She stuck her tiny fingers under the door, trying to grasp what light there was. Again she skimmed both hands up the wooden door, and finally, finally finding the handle, she jerked open the door. The TV illuminated the hallway, brightening her doorway. Dandy glanced over her shoulder; the hummcies retreated under her bed. She ran down the hall towards the living room. Dandy was safe. For now.

Daddy was asleep on the couch. His knees were tucked up close to his stomach. He looked like a baby sleeping there. Dandy wedged herself between the back of the couch and his curled-up legs. There were scratches on her feet and ankles. She pulled her nightgown over her knees.

As long as the TV was on, the hummcies would stay away. Even if they managed to turn off the TV, she figured Daddy would be too big for them. It would take a lot of hummcies to get through him. She wondered how many lived under crawl space. Dandy didn't want to think about that anymore, so she watched TV instead.

The news was playing. The Hillside Strangler had struck again. Two more bodies were found. The girls' names were Sonja Johnson and Dolores Johnson, fourteen and twelve years old. They attended St. Ignatius. On the day the girls went missing, they had gone shopping together at the Eagle Plaza. Two little boys found their bodies . . . left on a hill for eight days . . . .

She didn't remember running back to her room, but she awoke the following morning in her bedroom with the lights on and Mommy shaking her awake. Maybe Daddy carried her back. When he did that, he would say, "Night fairies flew you back. I told them you could stay with me, but they insisted you belonged in your bed. That they would watch over you."

Dandy rubbed sleep out of her eyes and told Mommy what happened. "The hummcies came again, but I made it to Daddy and then the night fairies put me back and protected me."

"Uh-huh. Yep. You get this shit from your Daddy." Mommy glanced at her wristwatch and said something Dandy couldn't hear under her breath. "Time to get up, Dandy. Your clothes are laid out. Call me when your shoes are on, and I'll help you tie them. There's a Pop-Tart in the toaster. And Gab," Mommy clapped her hands loudly over Gab's ears. "Up! I mean it!"

Before Dandy left for school, Mommy reminded her to come straight home and to not go outside. Mommy asked her what she was supposed to do when she got in, and Dandy, excited because she knew the answer, yelled "Lock the door behind me!" Then, to prove she was a big girl and knew her address, she counted out three and seven on her fingers and made a zero with her hand.

With her key in hand, Dandy sprinted out the front door to the sidewalk with her sisters behind her. It had rained just a little the night before, so everything looked especially clean. The grass was greener with the rain and morning dew.

She skipped down the sidewalk, occasionally checking to make sure the key was still in place. Dandy remembered her pretend horse and changed her gait to the horsey run. Dandy held the reins firmly in her hands, her horse galloping down the sidewalk at full speed.

The stop sign lady asked her why the rush, and Dandy told her she wanted to get to school so she could get back home. She had a key today. The lady said she was funny, told her it made sense, and took her across the street.

Throughout the day, Dandy touched her chest, fished out the yarn, and clasped her key in her hand until it hurt. It wasn't really playing with it because she made sure no one saw it. Except for one time she showed her friend, Jenny. Jenny wanted to wear it, so she let her, but only for twenty seconds, and they both counted to twenty at the same time.

At recess, she fell hard on the black rubber surface under the jungle gym. It knocked the air out of her. Dandy had never felt this sensation before so she lay on her back for some time, wanting to cry, but not being able to breathe. The fifth graders would make fun of her, so she stayed on her back until the black rubber burned through her shirt. No one came to check on her. Someone normally came when one of the kids fell, but no one came and no one asked, so she got up and brushed off the bits of gravel and dust from her clothes.

Dandy realized the key had come out of her shirt. Frightened it may have been lost, she grasped the key in her small, little-girl hand, feeling for its protective power before putting it back under her shirt.

When school got out, Dandy was ready with her key. When the final bell rang, she jumped out of her seat and ran to the door. She wasn't supposed to run. Somewhere in the distance, she heard her teacher calling for her to stop and get in line, but the door was already open.

At the school gate, she squeezed between kids and made it out the other end to the sidewalk. Passing a crowd of kids getting onto buses, Dandy walked the length of the chain-link fence surrounding the playground, all the while clutching the piece of yarn around her neck. She was following some kids who went in the same direction as her house when she heard a voice call her name. She turned to the familiar voice of her friend, Maria Elena Malvado, who was standing on the other side of the fence.

"Hi."

"Hi."

"Want to play hopscotch?" Maria Elena Malvado pointed to the chalk boxes drawn on the concrete. Dandy liked to say Maria Elena Malvado's name in her head because she thought she was speaking Spanish.

"I can't. I'm supposed to go home."

"Okay." Maria Elena Malvado turned to go back to the game.

Dandy repeated, "I'm supposed to go straight home." She was supposed to go straight home but didn't want to. She wanted to play. She never got to play hopscotch. The kids in afterschool played it every day, but she always had to meet the neighbor.

She watched the girls jump and laugh and throw their trinkets their mommies had given them to play with. Some tossed quarters and nickels; pennies were too small. One girl had the dog from a Monopoly game. Dandy recognized it because she was never allowed to play with the pieces from the game, even when she promised to not lose them. She was jealous of these girls who got to play. She thought, *no one's home to play with me today.*

In one hand, Dandy clutched her key. With her other, she held onto the gray metal chain-link fence that felt more like prison bars now, keeping her away from fun. This may be her only chance to play today, and she had something better than a nickel or a tiny silver car to toss. She had her key.

She called out, "Maria!" No one knew Dandy's secret name game; Maria didn't even know because Dandy always called her by her first name.

The gate to the playground locked from the inside, so Maria Elena Malvado let Dandy in. Maria Elena Malvado threw her nickel, jumped one-footed to the box where her nickel lay, and jumped back. Dandy threw her key, but the string got in the way. Maria Elena Malvado said she was in between squares, so she was supposed to throw again. She went back to the beginning, where the other girls were nudging each other, and threw it. This time, though, another girl said it was her turn, and Dandy had cut the line. The girl ran to Dandy's key and picked it up.

"That's mine. Give it back."

"No, you're a cheater. Cheaters don't get to play." The girl was older and bigger than Dandy.

"That's my key! It's mine!" This time she shouted at the girl.

The girl hopped around her like she was part of the game. She twirled the string around her finger, right in Dandy's face.

"Do you want it?"

Twirl, twirl, twirl. Dandy followed her key with her eyes.

"How bad do you want it, baby? You know you're a big baby. Does your mommy always make you wear your key? Ever hear of a keychain, dummy, baby dummy?"

She sang, "Big baby, big baby, dummy baby, baby." A few older girls heard and came over to sing it too until Dandy cried and yelled between sobs, "Give it back, give it back, it's mine!"

From nowhere, a woman appeared and broke up the girls. She asked Dandy who she was, what she was doing there.

Dandy calmed down enough to tell her that she was walking home, but Maria Elena Malvado asked her to play hopscotch. The lady looked over at Maria Elena Malvado, who shrugged and acted like she didn't know Dandy. The woman told Dandy to follow her and checked her chart with the afterschool kids' names on it to make sure she wasn't one of hers. The lady confirmed Dandy didn't belong to her and asked her where she lived. She told Dandy to hurry up and next time to go straight home. She made the mean girl give her key back and walked Dandy to the gate to make sure she got back to the sidewalk.

When Dandy was through the gate and the woman was on the other side, she turned right like the woman told her to do and started to walk, but she didn't know the buildings. When the lady asked her if this was the way she got home, she said yes, but only because she thought she was supposed to say yes. The lady seemed to know where she lived.

Dandy made little sobbing sounds. Something told her to go back, so she turned around and ran back to the gate. The woman was already far across the playground. There was no way back in.

There were more kids coming in her direction, though, and Maria Elena Malvado was amongst them. A couple of the mean girls were in the group too, but not the main one, so she waited and leaned against the fence. The bigger kids swept past her.

Maria Elena Malvado stopped in front of her and said, "I'm sorry."

Dandy said, "Okay."

"Are you going home?"

"Yes. I don't know the way."

Maria Elena Malvado giggled. "I do."

"You do?"

"Maria, Marrrrriaaaa!" A boy with a skateboard yelled her name. "Come on!"

"Coming."

Maria ran, calling over her shoulder to Dandy, "You coming?"

They caught up with the boy, who Maria Elena Malvado said was her brother. The two spoke Spanish. Dandy understood some of the words, *escuela, casa, nina*, but nothing else. The boy acted mad. He stopped walking, looked down at Dandy, and said, "You can't come home with us, you know? Why you following us? Where's your home?"

She was hurt. She wasn't following. Maria Elena Malvado knew the way. She told the boy, "Three, seven, zero, Dunrobin."

"*Muchacha*, you're on the wrong side of the block. You're behind the school. *Poco idiota.* I bet you don't even know where you are. *Maria, te vas a casa.* Come on. I'll show you."

Maria Elena Malvado stopped walking next to Dandy and ran into an apartment building. The boy took her to the end of the block, pointed to a sign, and said, "Walk over there and wait for the lady." He turned away from her and skated back to the apartments.

Dandy walked to the end of the street and read the sign. Imperial Highway. She recognized the word "Imperial" because Mommy said it before and had pointed the sign out to her. She was on the right sidewalk now and would be home soon.

She stood on the crosswalk and squinted against the sun, scanning the sidewalk and street for the crosswalk lady. "DON'T WALK" appeared in bright orange lights on the sign across the street. She looked and looked and when she finally saw her, Dandy noticed the lady was no longer wearing her neon vest. She was walking further away from her like she didn't belong to the sidewalk.

"WALK" appeared in white letters now, but Dandy had never walked across the street without someone else. She watched cars sailing across the four lanes of traffic to their destinations—Imperial Highway now the Pacific Ocean. Red car, brown car, black car. She counted them in her head. So many she couldn't even count that high. There was no getting across, so she stood on her piece of the island clinging to the hot metal of the light pole, frozen at the possibility of crossing Imperial. She considered going back to where she saw Maria Elena Malvado go in, but she was too scared to leave this spot that was so close to home.

Dandy had never been alone before. She felt for her key—the only thing keeping her from harm. If she could just get home. She grasped the piece of metal in her tiny fist and prayed it did not get dark, prayed the hummcies weren't sniffing her out. She wanted to keep her soul.

If she had her daddy, none of this would have happened. It roared through her head. *I want my daddy. I want my daddy. I want my daddy.* She wanted to yell for him. *Daddy, Daddy.* But she did not yell. Instead, she stood on the dusty sidewalk that was supposed to take her home.

Fear oozed out of the sidewalk and wrapped its dark cloak around her. It folded her into its will, into its murky clutches. Dandy felt all the bad things she'd done, and she was *so* sorry. She *was* a bad girl. She *didn't* go straight home. She never slept in her bed like Mommy told her to do. She should want her mommy, like all other kids would, but instead she wanted Daddy and she thought, *Mommy knows. Mommy knows I love Daddy more, and this is why I can't get home.*

She hugged the light post, the street's sorry surrogate for her daddy. Tears streamed down her face. All was lost without Daddy. And then, a man with a moustache like her daddy's walked up and stood next to her. The man was bald.

The man looked at her funny. He glanced up the street then peered down at her again.

Dandy kept her head down because she knew not to talk to strangers. If she looked up, he would try to talk to her. She smeared her tears across her face with her sweaty palms and tried to focus on the gutter with its broken glass, bottle caps, candy wrappers, and cigarette butts. She had to pee.

The light changed. "WALK." The man began to walk across the street. Dandy knew she ought to go too but couldn't move because she wasn't allowed to go anywhere with strangers.

The man stopped halfway across the street, turned around, and asked, "Are you lost, little girl? Where are you supposed to be?"

Because she wasn't supposed to talk, she pointed across the street in the direction he was walking. He came back.

"What are you doing here? This is a busy street."

She pointed to the deserted school behind her.

"Is someone coming to get you?"

Dandy shook her head no.

"Are you lost?"

She shook her head no again.

"Do you live near here?"

She pointed back across the street.

The light changed a second time. "DON'T WALK." The speeding cars blew warm wind against the fuzzy blonde hair on her legs.

"Do you have a name?"

Dandy nodded yes.

"Oh, I see. I'm a stranger. You can't talk to me, right?"

The man was nodding his head as if he understood everything now. Dandy wondered if he knew her parents. It was what Mommy and Daddy said, and he knew it too. She felt a little better.

"Did your mommy and daddy tell you that?"

She nodded yes again.

"It's good advice, but sometimes you have to talk to strangers because they can help you. You can talk to me. We're not all bad. I'm a good guy."

He knelt on the sidewalk to get closer to her face. Dandy tried not to look at his bald head. He said, "You're pretty. I bet you hear that all the time, but this isn't a safe place for you. I'm Levi. What's your name?"

She was stuck. This wasn't a question she could nod yes or no to. Levi was smiling into her eyes now. She felt she had to tell him, so she did, but kept her head down.

"See? Now we're friends. We know each other's names. You can trust me. You're lucky I'm not one of those bad men your parents told you about because, believe me, they're out here. Do you know the way?"

Levi held out his hand for her to hold as they crossed the street. His hand was smooth, not rough like Daddy's. When they made it across, he asked her what her address was. Dandy told him even though something inside her told her not to. He held her hand the entire way home. It felt odd, a stranger touching her, but she didn't want to make him sad by pulling her hand away.

On the way, Levi asked her if she liked Disneyland. He asked her what her favorite ride was. Dandy answered all his questions, comforted someone was taking care of her now.

Levi told her he liked Disneyland, too. Maybe they could go together sometime. His favorite ride was the Haunted Mansion. Did she think it was too scary? She told him no. He acted surprised and asked how she knew. She told him Mommy said the ghosts weren't real. Levi asked her if they weren't real, how did they get in your rollercoaster ride? She thought maybe they were real after all even though Mommy said they weren't, but Mommy didn't believe in hummcies or night fairies and Dandy knew those were real. Dandy wanted to ask more about the ghosts now, but Levi said, "We shouldn't talk about stuff like that. You're too young. It'll give you nightmares. Why are you by yourself?"

She didn't know how to answer him, but they were in her driveway now.

"Is anyone home waiting for you inside?"

Dandy didn't want to say, but Levi gripped her hand harder as if he wouldn't let go without an answer. Dandy told him Mommy was coming home soon and that she had a key. He asked her where her key was, and she showed him the yarn around her neck. He pulled the yarn out from under her shirt. His fingernails grazed the indentation in her neck where she had been pulling the yarn earlier.

Levi told her she needed to be more careful in the future because there were bad men who lived in the boarded-up houses around here. They might have gotten her if he hadn't rescued her.

Then Levi told her he lived nearby and that they were neighbors. He asked if he looked familiar. He said it would be safer for her to come with him, at least until her mommy got home. Then, he'd take her back to her house.

He started asking a lot of questions. What time does your Mommy come home? Dandy didn't remember. Do you always walk home by yourself? No, the neighbor. Where's your daddy? At work. Do you have a sister? Yes, two. How old are they? Twelve and thirteen. He asked so many questions at one time that Dandy got confused. She wanted to leave, but Levi was still holding her hand.

Levi knelt on both knees. His face was so close to hers she could smell his chewing gum. He offered her a piece but said he'd give it to her when they got to his place. She'd call Mommy, he would give Mommy his address to pick her up, then he'd give her some gum.

Dandy didn't know why she had to go with Levi when her house was right there. *If he would just let go of my hand*, she thought. She didn't like how near Levi was to her and how he wouldn't let go of her hand as though she belonged to him. She didn't like his eyes, either. They didn't look happy, sad, mean, nice, nothing. They were nothing eyes like the predatory eyes of Mommy's kitty, April, when it was stalking a bug or a squirrel. Levi was scaring her.

A door slammed, and Shelli and Brian—the neighbor kids—ran out. They were teenagers and went to high school. Shelli was her babysitter, but Mommy said now that Amy was thirteen they didn't need Shelli anymore. Shelli waved at Dandy, and Dandy waved back.

Then Shelli started to get into her car but stopped and asked Dandy what she was doing.

"I'm going home," Dandy said.

"Where's your mom?" Shelli asked.

"At work?"

"But Gab and Amy are there, right?"

"No."

Shelli got a worried look on her face. "Who are you?" Shelli asked Levi.

Levi stood up abruptly, released Dandy's hand, and handed her key back. He didn't tell Shelli his name.

"His name is Levi," Dandy said.

"How do you know him?" Shelli asked while staring at Levi.

Levi didn't let Dandy answer. He said, "She was lost. I brought her home."

"Well, she's home now, so you can go," Brian said.

"Get inside," Shelli told her.

"Mister, you got a thing for little girls?" Brian asked, "You got about ten seconds before I call the police."

Dandy didn't understand. She wondered if she would get in trouble. If Shelli and Brian would tell on her for walking with a stranger. Dandy ran to the front door.

At the door, Dandy stopped to see if Levi was still at the end of her driveway. He was, and he was arguing with Shelli and Brian saying, "I didn't do anything wrong. I didn't do anything," over and over. He seemed upset, but then Brian said, "If you didn't do anything wrong, then you can tell the police all about it." Levi left then, walking away quickly.

Shelli called after her. "Don't talk to strangers. There's been bad things happening around here to girls."

Dandy recalled the news, the girls, but those were those girls, not her.

Dandy unlocked the door, entered, and shut and locked the door like Mommy told her to do. She dropped her bookbag on the tile floor. Light filtering through closed shades gave the living room a shadowy effect. There was music playing. Bad music. James Bond's "Goldfinger," the song she hated more than any other song in the whole world, was playing on the record player. Her sisters played it when her parents went out and would chase her through the house yelling that Mr. Goldfinger was going to get her. She told Mommy, and they got in trouble for it.

Dandy knew she wasn't alone.

Instinct told her to get out, to go no further, but she was home, and it had taken so much to get here. It had to be her sisters. If they didn't hear her come in, she could make it to the back door and climb the plum tree.

She committed to inching forward, soundless on her tiptoes. When both feet were planted on the brown and gold shag carpet, she arched, ready to launch her body with full force to the kitchen, where the back door was, but she heard something murmuring. Pleading sounds came from behind the couch. It sounded like Mommy, like she was hurt. Dandy turned in the direction of the voice. In the moment it took her to face its piteous appeals, an enormous hummcie staggered from behind the couch. She'd never seen a human-sized hummcie. She didn't know they got so big, but it was there in front of her. Its mouth gaped open, exposing uneven serrated teeth. It swayed back and forth with its arms beckoning her to come into its embrace. "Come play with me," it called.

Dandy screamed, ran, and tore through the living room as fast as she'd ever run, but the hummcie was quicker and swept her up.

Squirming, she broke free. Its horrific hiss called out again to her. She made it to the back door and pulled on the handle to the screen door. It was locked. The hummcie had her now. It picked her up, biting her arms, shoulders, neck. She bit it back—hard. On the shoulder. The hummcie yelped and dropped her. Dandy sprinted towards her room.

She slammed her bedroom door, but it didn't have a lock; her parents wouldn't allow it. She would have to hide. *But where?* She didn't have a closet, only a wardrobe full of her and Gab's stuff. There was nowhere. She heard the hummcie thundering down the hall. Dandy had no choice. She snatched Sunny Bear off her bed and dove beneath it. It was dark under there, but she could manage a few small hummcies.

She heard the hummcie walking towards the edge of the bed, saw its bare feet from beneath her bed skirt. It had human feet with painted toenails. The hummcie knelt down, lifted the bed skirt, and said, "Dandy, it's me. It's Mommy." Mommy removed the plastic teeth from her mouth. "It's Mommy. See? I'm sorry. I managed to get out early. I was just playing. I didn't know you wouldn't recognize me."

By this time, the record player had started a new song, and Dandy understood Mommy was pretending. Mommy handed Dandy the set of fake vampire teeth like a consolation prize and said, "Here, you can have them. It was just a joke, honey. I didn't mean to scare you."

The plastic teeth were still wet from Mommy's mouth. Dandy's face was covered in snot and salty tears. Her shirt was soaked in sweat. She had peed a little on herself.

From under the bed, Dandy glared at Mommy. She understood—a joke.

"Come on, come out from there."

"*No.*"

"Come on. You can have ice cream."

"I don't want any."

Dandy hugged Sunny Bear close. She wasn't afraid anymore. She'd made it home, but she felt a hollowness in her tummy she'd never felt before, as though the hummcies had gotten a little chunk of her soul. The no one coming to help her when she fell, the mean hopscotch girls, getting lost, Levi, now Mommy. Mommy, who she was supposed to trust. Dandy was mad.

"Alright then. When you're ready. I'm sorry, Dandy."

Dandy watched Mommy's feet and ankles leave her room. She let go of Sunny Bear and studied the fake fangs Mommy gave her. She grasped them tightly together into a fist. Then it occurred to her that maybe Mommy wasn't really Mommy. She'd wondered about it before. Maybe Mommy had a hummcie in her and no one knew it and that's why she sometimes did mean things to Dandy.

She watched as one withered finger poked through the carpeting, then another, and another. She squeezed the fangs even harder. She counted three shrunken heads, four, six. When nine curved, miniature spines pushed through the carpeting, flailing anorexic arms, chanting, *Come play with us*, like they always did, she crushed the fake fangs into her hand. They weren't sharp enough to pierce her skin, but she understood enough now to know hummcies weren't the real danger. A lot of hummcies could be a problem, but Dandy was bigger, stronger, and smarter than them.

Dandy let the hummcies get almost all the way out before she savagely kicked one, then two, snapping their brittle bones. One crawled up her arm. She squeezed its neck until its head popped off. She wiped goo from her hand onto the carpeting. A few she kicked out from under the bed. They shriveled into husks. The sunlight from her window ate up their empty bodies. Some howled at her and scurried back down into the crawl space. When they got the nerve to come back up, she smashed a few more. Yet, more came, and even more as if there was an anthill in the crawlspace with an endless supply of hummcies. Killing hummcies was fun after all, and Dandy said, "I like playing with you. I have another friend who wants to play too."

Who, who?

Hummcies are dumb babies, Dandy thought.

Dandy grabbed Sunny Bear and rolled out from underneath her bed. She shut her blinds and curtains so the hummcies could safely travel. There must have been fifty, maybe more, following her down the hallway.

"Wait here," she told them. They hovered in a dark corner of the hallway.

Dandy could smell ground beef cooking. She knew Mommy was in the kitchen. She shut the blinds and the curtains in Mommy and Daddy's room.

She lifted the bed skirt and said, "Here." She pointed under the bed. "Her name is Mommy and she's a big, big demon." Daddy always slept on the couch, so Dandy would sneak from her room tonight and sleep out there with him when Mommy went to bed.

An army of hummcies traveled from under Dandy's bed and through the hallway, finally gathering under Mommy's bed. Dandy flipped the light switch on and off like Mommy did to her last night, just in case they got any ideas. They hissed, *No light, no light.*

There were so many. It made them move faster. Several got caught by the light and shriveled into crusty shells of themselves. She picked up the withered bodies and tossed them under the bed so the live hummcies could gnaw on their bones, chew on their tough skin.

She ignored their pleas and knelt beside the edge of the bed to look at what she had created. Hundreds and hundreds of hummcies crowded under Mommy's bed. They rubbed their veiny, bruised-looking hands together gleefully and chanted, *We get to play with Mommy, with Mommy.*

"Mommy forgot who she is. It's time for her to go back with you now, but Mommy doesn't believe in hummcies," Dandy told them.

She will, she will, she will.

Dandy stood up, satisfied. She turned off the bedroom light and went to pee.

Playing With Dolls

by Maria Klouda

The crow is back. Every day it struts in front of the house as if to tell me it knows what I've done.

It jumps to the curb and walks in a circle, never taking flight, following the lines of the cul-de-sac, pecking at the ground. Watching me.

My crow is beautiful. The early morning sun reflects the purple hidden in the black feathers, reminding me of the color of a bruise. The kind that forms when he strikes you.

The bones in the yard lie only a few feet away. I don't hear them rattling anymore. Not like at the beginning.

I was meeting Ollie to return a borrowed book. I arrived at the cafe first and ordered my coffee and blueberry muffin. Customers crowded the patio, so I grabbed a table and waited. It wasn't long before she joined me outside.

I slid the old, worn book across the table to her. The cover was blank. Black. "Finished, it was . . . interesting. I have a funny story to share," I said.

"Yay? How are things with you-know-who?" she sarcastically answered as if she wasn't quite sure she wanted to hear the tale. We had been talking a lot lately. Not much had been funny.

Two conversations were in progress, and we both kept up with the other.

"About the same," I began. She was asking about him, the bruise-giver. I wanted to share the story instead. "I worked my shift at the tutoring center on Tuesday. One of the students got on the topic of vampires. She went on to say that she wanted to marry a vampire. She wondered if vampires could reproduce."

Ollie was amused but remained silent.

"The whole room had a very long discussion on the possibilities of reproduction among vampires. We traced the origins of vampires back to Greek mythology and the curse of Ambrogio. The consensus of the students and faculty was that only sparkly vampires could reproduce if their partner were mortal. You know, Edward and Bella. Look," I showed her a picture on my phone.

She leaned over to get a better look at the tiny screen. We both laughed.

"Is that a vampire equation?" Ollie asked, looking up from the phone. She added, "You need protection spells and talismans around that junk. I'll get that for you since I'm a master of protective charms. You must have some spiritual protection of your own to survive this debacle and still be able to have a presence at that place. If you can get me some personal items, I can help you. I can make a poppet."

I placed the phone back on the table.

"Yea, she drew a Punnet Square. It has something to do with

cross-breeding experiments. We even posted on Twitter and tagged Stephanie Myer. Another student joined in and pointed out that she thought it was significant that vampires originated with a curse. I wondered if that was the case, why hasn't the curse been reversed? No one answered, and we all left for classes."

"Wow! That's some intellectual dialogue you had going on. It's amusing how kids think." Ollie seemed distracted and was rummaging through her purse as if looking for something.

I continued, "Later, I asked the students in my class, and they voted pretty much the same way. A few thought it could be feasible, but most agreed it was impossible for vampires to reproduce because they are technically no longer living, so their organs wouldn't work. One student, who had been taking this all in, finally spoke up and said it depends on the strain of vampire, that he thinks some could. We laughed and agreed again—it could only be the sparkly ones."

Ollie looked at me, wondering if that was the end of the story. I took a sip of coffee and held up a hand, indicating more was to come.

"I went on to explain the curse and asked the same question I had before about someone reversing the curse. I kid you not, at that very moment, the door to the classroom closed. I laughed it off and started class."

"Wait, the door closed by itself?" Ollie was alarmed. I nodded yes. "Any other instances?"

"Not unless thinking how ugly a rug is and then accidentally spilling coffee on it counts?" I shrugged.

Ollie laughed, "No, I think that was just you projecting your negative feelings towards the carpet and, in a very Freudian way, spilling your coffee."

"OK. So what now? Do you make anything of it? The door?" I asked.

"What building were you in? I'll tell you that I picked up on some bad stuff in one building when I visited a class last spring. I wanted out of that place. It was near the entrance to campus." Ollie rubbed her forearms as if to wipe away chill bumps.

"That has to be the PJ. Spirits haunt the building," I confirmed. "Years ago, a janitor hung himself in the attic. You can hear the nightly sounds of a rope swinging coming from the padlocked attic."

"It was a deliberately confusing building. We walked up, then down. The class was on the lower level. I'm sensitive to stuff like that, and I couldn't wait to get the fuck out. I never mentioned it to anyone. Most people aren't keen on my skills. Even when I offer to help them, they are too scared to dabble in the craft. Anyway, it had this energy that sucked the life out of me. I couldn't think straight."

Later, I would remember the afternoon as a recruiting meeting, but it was not clear which of us was recruiting the other.

"I can see it might be hard for some people to process," I confirmed. The conversation had shifted.

"They are scared it might come back to them or something. That's not the way it works."

I nodded, coming back to the earlier suggestion. "What's a poppet?"

She explained that a poppet is kind of like a voodoo doll. It's the spiritual representation of whomever you intend it to be, so when you create one, you need a lot of personal items from the person you are making.

I recall my high school friend who had a voodoo doll. I never thought much of it other than a way to take out frustrations based on other people's actions. "Stick a pin in the dolly," we joked.

Ollie explained, "Voodoo dolls are just effigies of people and have specific purposes. The difference with the poppet is that it actually stands in for the person. So, you can get some of the personal items of the person and create actions towards them. Make sense?"

I hesitated. Thinking.

"Shit. I freaked you out. Sorry!" Ollie said.

I nodded, "No, not really."

When I was in high school, the guy I had been dating for a while asked me to prom. I bought the dress, and the week before the prom, he canceled on me, and we broke up. He had gotten back together with an ex-girlfriend, and they were going to the prom.

Devastated and rejected. I told my friend what had happened, and she put a pin in the voodoo doll's leg for him. The following weekend, he was waterskiing at the lake with some friends. He took a nasty fall and broke his ankle. No prom for him either.

I'm not sure if I believe or that I don't not believe. I mean, I'm open to accepting the possibilities. For now, I am a captive audience.

She continued, "You have no idea how excited I am about this. It'll be way more effective if we make his poppet together because of the energy we can put into it. Don't you work near him? It doesn't have to be big items or items he will miss. Does he brush his hair? Hair and nails are ideal. Just give his office a once over. I have his signature already, but I need more. Does he have a jacket or an item of clothing that he wouldn't miss?"

I couldn't be anywhere near him. He who inflicted pain. His office gave me the heebie-jeebies.

As if she knew what I was thinking, "You don't have to be with him. . . see what you can get your hands on." She paused, "You have to be careful. Negative energy from multiple sources is destructive. We can focus on energy work. Put what you want into the universe, and it will happen. I don't feel bad about returning negative energy when it was originally given to me. It's only fair." I was not the only one he had hurt.

Ollie changes the subject, "I can read your tarot. I know a decent medium. Remember, I convene with the dead. Cemeteries hold knowledge. We have to be willing to listen."

"I've always been afraid to get a tarot reading," I admit.

"Why?"

I shrug, "Scared it would be a slap of reality. I might let you, though. Maybe help put some things into perspective. Have I told you about the bones in the side yard?"

"Bones? You have a connection to the earth. Not the planet, the dirt."

"The dirt—I like that."

Where secrets are buried.

It was time to go.

We cleared our table of trash and hugged goodbye.

We never made the poppet together, and she didn't read my tarot. But a seed had been planted. Magical connections and asking the universe for guidance. Why not? I thought. What harm could come from a wish?

One afternoon, as I pulled out of the parking lot, he crossed the road in front of me. Glancing down at his phone as he walked, he remained oblivious to his surroundings. I waited for the others to clear the lane, and somehow, he was the only person left in my path. I briefly considered punching the gas and barreling over him. I made a joke about the benefits of Subaru's All-Wheel Drive capabilities. And, I did nothing. He hopped onto the sidewalk and continued on his way.

Playing With Dolls

The pin in the doll's neck remained where I had put it the day he hit me.

They found him later in the padlocked attic of the PJ building, where he had hung himself.

———

The crow takes flight and lands on the branch of the gnarled tree in the yard. It gifts me with a harsh caw that carries in the wind off the mountain. I am safe.

CONTRIBUTORS

Greg Bhatia
Facebook: @wizowords

Mark Braught
Instagram: @markbraught
Facebook: @mark.braught
Website: www.markbraught.com

Emma Cariello
Twitter: @EmmaRoseCari

Alyssa Hamilton
Twitter: @AnnWandering
Instagram: @annwandering

Ann Hite
Twitter: @annhite
Instagram: @annhiteauthor
Facebook: @AnnHite

Annie James
Twitter: @charmony777
Instagram: @annie.james.author
Facebook: @anniejamesauthor

Maria Klouda
Website: www.clippings.me/
mariaklouda

Dawn Major
Twitter: @Dwritable
Instagram: @dwriteable
Facebook: @dawn.major.50
Website: www.dawnmajor.com

Bonnie Medford
Twitter: @Bonnie_Writes
Instagram: @bonnies_literary_obsession

Ben Meeks
Instagram: @authorbenmeeks
Facebook: @AuthorBenMeeks
Website: www.authorbenmeeks.com

Austin C. Nichols
Instagram: @ac_nichols

Lincoln Reed
Twitter: @LincolnPReed
Facebook: @lincoln.reed.3
Website: www.lincolnreedonline.com

Kristen Reid
Twitter: @Kris10BelleReid
Instagram: @writerkristenreid
Website: linktr.ee/kris10reid

Juliet Rose
Instagram: @authorjulietrose
Facebook: @authorjulietrose
Website: www.authorjulietrose.com

Jon Sokol
Twitter: @JonSokolWriter
Instagram: @jonsokol_writer
Website: www.jonsokol.com

Acknowledgements

Springer Mountain Press would like to thank all of the contributors who helped build this anthology. Without you, this book wouldn't exist, so thank you again.

We would also like to thank visiting editor CBM for all of her hard work in making this publication possible. Her help was truly invaluable.

And a special thank you goes out to Springer Mountain Press employees Sarah Fulton and Taylor Knecht for your assistance and support on the Anthology.

SPRINGER MOUNTAIN PRESS

Instagram: @springernountainpress
Twitter: @SpringerMtPress
Facebook: @springermountainpress